Father, Daughter, and Lover

In the light of dawn they walked slowly and in silence across the damp fields. As they reached Margaret's home, her father ran out to meet them. His face was black with rage. He glanced at Margaret with such scorn that she flinched, but his business was with John. He brandished his fist in the younger man's face.

"So that's how you want my gal, is it?" he shouted. "Keepin' her out all night doin' God knows what, except you know! And I know, too!"

Margaret rushed between the two men. Her father raised his fist and smashed it into her face. She staggered, felt blood pouring from her mouth and nose. She sank down to the ground on her hands and knees.

Dimly she heard roars, shouts, thuds. She could not see yet. She felt herself lifted, felt a gentle hand wiping the blood from her eyes.

"All right, Maggie?" asked John in a thickened voice. "I'll kill him for this, by God, I will!"

Other books by Taylor Caldwell:

THIS SIDE OF INNOCENCE
DYNASTY OF DEATH
THE DEVIL'S ADVOCATE

MAGGIE — HER MARRIAGE

A Gold Medal Original
by

Taylor Caldwell

GOLD MEDAL BOOKS

FAWCETT PUBLICATIONS, Inc., NEW YORK

MAGGIE—HER MARRIAGE

Chapter One

PETER HAMILTON, who was no fool, often remarked at "Good Book readin' time" that there was nothing in the Bible, not even in Genesis, that indicated God "thought." God "did." Of course, nothing that Peter Hamilton said was of any account to his neighbors, just as all the Hamiltons were considered to be permanent liabilities to the community. So Peter's favorite remark on the activities of the Almighty was dismissed as "blasphemy" and worthy of a man held in low esteem. This did not bother Peter, for his opinion of his community was as low as its opinion of him.

He loved his smithy because he loved sweat and the rhythm of his strong muscles. Nothing was very important to him except the joy of his labor. It was a full expression of all of him, of his body, his mind, and his healthy sexuality. He was forty-two years old, twenty-two years married, the husband of an enfeebled hypochondriac, the father of five living children and five dead children. He was poor and jovial, boisterous and animal, given to brutalities like those of the earth he loved.

This warm autumn day inspired him to increased efforts. Occasionally he paused to get his breath and look over the hazy heat of the countryside. The sky was pale and warm and dazzling; the hills were folded ridges of bronze, the fields had a patina of rough gold. He heard the restless cawing of crows, the stamping of the horses. Otherwise there was no sound; there was only heat and dazzle.

He slowly came out of the black and flaming cavern of the smithy and stood in the doorway, wiping his hands on his leather apron, yawning for several minutes. He lit his pipe, pushing in the tobacco with a black thumb. He yawned again, glanced at the sky.

"Phew! It's hot today!" he exclaimed. The horse pricked up his ears, rolled an affectionate eye at him. Heat waves danced over the harvested fields, shimmered in the foliage of the burning maples.

The blacksmith flexed his great arms, enjoying the strength of them. He rubbed his beard with the back of his hand; even the feel of the strong bristles against his rough skin gave him pleasure. Then he stood listening alertly. Hoofbeats, muffled by the thick dust of the road, drummed through the silent air.

"Well, here comes your boss!" he said to the horse, slapping him on the back. The horse pricked up his ears, turned restlessly toward the sound of the coming hoofbeats. An amiable expression spread over Peter's face; he looked expectantly up the road. A horseman came in sight around the bend, a mighty horseman on a mightier horse. He cantered rapidly up to the blacksmith, reined in competently, and smiled down at the man below.

"Phew! Hotter'n hell," he announced. "Hoss shod?"

"Yep. Here he be, John."

"Well," said the horseman. "How much do I owe you?"

The price was named and received. The jingle of the coins was loud in the stillness. The man on the horse seemed to reflect.

He was a young man, still under thirty, taller and broader than Peter. He had a strong face, with the short distended nose of the belligerent man, a firmly cut mouth, and keen direct eyes. His ears were burned scarlet, but his complexion was a rich brown accented by low, black brows and black hair. His shoulders were exceptionally broad, his torso magnificent. Despite the thick dust on his clothing, it was evident that he was a man of substance, for his coat was well cut, of good broadcloth.

He was John Hobart, owner of four hundred acres of rich black bottom land, stockman and amateur banker, final word in the local Baptist Church, politician and arbiter of manners and morals, consulted on practically everything. No one in that community dared defy him. No farmer would have dreamed of buying a new breed of hog or cow without consulting him; his opinion was deferentially asked on all matters from weddings to crops. If he were arrogant and brusque, his opinion was invariably sound, compounded of belief in his own infallibility and real intelligence. He was a shrewd, practical man, softened by impulses of charity, which he often regretted later.

"Looks as though we might have a good rain," said Peter, just to make conversation.

"Bah," said Hobart, squinting at the sky. "Ain't goin' to be any rain for a long time. You town folks never know nothin' about the weather."

Looked at broadly, Peter was not a townsman, though his twenty acres stood not more than two miles from Whitmore, the county seat, a town of about ten thousand inhabitants. But the twenty acres did not entirely support his family, and, therefore, he was a "townsman."

John's immediate dismissal of his opinion riled the blacksmith. He had not really believed that any rain portended. But he was as elemental as nature, and his quick blood rose to his face. So he deliberately, with a hidden confidence of a certain power he had over the younger man, lifted his face to the burning heavens.

"An' I say there *will* be rain soon," he almost shouted. "Maybe tomorrow. Tomorrow night, sure. You wait and see."

"Bah," said John again, and he spat into the dust. Conversation languished.

"Look here!" John burst out suddenly, his broad face turning a deeper color. "How about that gal of yours, Maggie? How long do I have to wait? Ain't she made up her mind yet?"

Peter turned childlike eyes upon John. Inwardly he was gloating.

"Ain't asked her lately," he said. "Tell you what, 'spose you come 'round tonight and ask her yourself? Come to supper."

John wrinkled his nose in frank distaste, thinking of Peter's home.

"No, thanks," he said shortly, and wheeled his horse. He would have ridden off then, but there was Maggie. At the thought of her, his red ears went crimson. Why, hundreds of women, even those who lived twenty miles away in the state capital, Williamsburg, would have trembled with joy if he had even crooked a finger at them. Doctors' daughters, too, girls with money, educated, and ladies. And he had to want Maggie Hamilton, a frowsy country wench, who lived among a swarm of children in a house little better than a hovel! He hated himself viciously; the next minute he knew that he must have her.

At first he had never dreamed of marrying her. He had set out to seduce her. She would not be seduced. Finally, in spite of his rage and self-contempt, he had proposed marriage. He had stared at her incredulously; finally, in a choked voice, he had asked her if she didn't love him. She had studied him thoughtfully, her eyes traveling as boldly over him as they might have traveled over a stallion. Then she admitted that she didn't know. But she had colored.

She must have time, she said. Time! A blacksmith's

daughter—! He had ridden away in a fury, vowing never to look at her again. But, that night, he had remembered her, and every molecule of his body had yearned for her. She was in his blood; she belonged to him. And he came back, drawn by something stronger than his will. She had not seemed surprised to see him. She had expected him. And she was continuing to torture him, damn her! Keeping him dangling; making a fool of him in the eyes of the astonished folk whom he regarded as thoroughly inferior.

He was not subtle enough to know why she hesitated. He knew that she liked him; when he took her hand she trembled. She had allowed him to kiss her a few times; he had felt the uncontrollable way in which she had pressed her round breast hard against his chest; he had felt in her an answering passion. And then, later, she had reiterated that she must have time. Why, in the name of God?

He was thinking of all these things as he sat in glowering silence on his restless horse. "What ails the gal, anyways?" he demanded. "Anyone else, or somethin'?"

Peter scratched his head, ruminating.

"No, there ain't no one else. See here, John, Maggie likes you. She told me so. But, she's allus been free and easy-like, runnin' around, goin' to see my old Grandmaw, and talkin' to her. Why, the ole woman taught Maggie to write and read all kinds of outlandish books she brought from England when she was a gal herself. We've got good blood in our family, even if I say it myself. The ole woman can speak three languages, too, she says, and figure like all get-out. Writes a hand like a scholar. Well, she's given Maggie notions. The gal told me only yesterday that gettin' married was serious and ought to be thought about. But, she likes you, John. It'll come out all right; no use gettin' het up about it."

The younger man allowed himself to be placated but he still scowled.

"What's this I bin hearin' lately about Maggie and that no-account cousin of her'n, Ralph Blodgett? Folks say she roams around with him, and I've—"

Peter burst out into a roar of honest laughter.

"That young dreamer," he jeered. "Why he's younger'n Maggie, and ain't even as tall as her. He and that silly ole mother of his! Time and time again I've told Melindy that there's cracked heads in her family, with that sister of hers mincin' around. She never let her ole man train the boy to run the farm proper, as you know, John, and they've got the measliest hunnerd acres this side of Whitmore. If it weren't for their hired man, they'd been thrown out long ago. And Ralph's just like her, always readin' and talkin' poetry to Maggie. The gal's just sorry for him, he bein' laughed at by all the folks in the county, and she stands up for him. But, as for marryin' that Ralph Blodgett—! Maggie's got sense."

John chewed his lip for some moments, relieved. Then he glared again at Peter.

"If you had an ounce of guts you'd talk to her proper, seein' as you're her dad."

Instantly Peter's face became congested with rage. He seized the reins of John's horse; his flaming black eyes assaulted the other.

"See here, John Hobart, you may be the big noise in this county, but no man's goin' to tell me I ain't got guts! Why, damn you, I kin whip you with one hand tied behind me."

They glared at each other. John clutched his whip; then he remembered that Peter was Maggie's father; moreover, he really admired the older man. He smiled darkly.

"Say— We're not goin' to fight, you and me, Pete. What for? I've allus said you're the smartest man in the county. What I meant was that seein' as you are her father, you could say somethin' to Maggie about her and me." His smile grew broader.

Peter was not easily placated. He released the reins. "Well, I'm not sayin' anythin' to Maggie," he declared flatly. "She kin have you or she needn't. We need her at home, anyways. Allus did say that Maggie was the only young un I had that was any account. You'll have to fight it out yourself with her. I'm not sayin'."

He knew this was hypocrisy. He had been "sayin' " for a long time to Maggie. She was his favorite child; this marriage was beyond any dream of splendor he had ever had. Lately he had shouted at her; she had shouted back. He loved her very much; sometimes he regretted that she was his daughter. He had no taboos of thought.

"Tell you what," said John disarmingly. "I'll ride over tonight and have it out with her. After supper. Pete Hamilton, you've got the only gal in the county I'd look at twice! You know what things are all about; you wasn't born yesterday. I've got to have that gal, if I've got to pick her up and run with her. I'm a man, Pete."

Peter smiled again; his good nature almost completely restored. Damn it, the gal would say yes that night or get a horsewhippin'!

Chapter Two

"AIN'T BUT THREE KINDS of flowers worth a tinker's damn," declared Grandma Margot Hamilton as she stooped her ancient bulk to strip off a few withered leaves from her rose bushes. "And they're roses, lilacs, and sweet locust."

Her cracked old voice and her words were full of a curious combination of ignorance, intelligence, and culture. At times, she might have been at home in a drawing room, despite her sun-darkened old face with its web of deep furrows and wrinkles; at other times she might have been merely an ancient crone with misshapen heavy body and ragged old clothes. Seventy years ago she had been as tall and strong and vital as Margaret Hamilton, her great-granddaughter; she still had height and dignity but she was bowed. Her skin was like rich but cracking leather; nearly ninety, her black hair was still thick, with hardly a streak of gray; under beetling brows like Peter's, her small black eyes were intelligent and shrewd. She had told her great-granddaughter that she hated most everything; humanity, cats, cities, polite conversation, children, preachers, and, especially, women. This hatred included Peter Hamilton's wife and his four other children. "Can't abide that woman and her brats!" Her only human exceptions were Peter and his daughter, Margaret. A terrible old woman, finding no sin unpardonable, and few virtues forgivable.

She had been born in 1782; this fall of 1872 would bring her ninetieth birthday. She and her young husband, Samuel Hamilton, her cousin, had come to the raw new land, and had experienced Indians, desolation, wars, hunger, drought, fever, death, and birth in that ancient old log cabin at the front of her garden. These bare golden hills were still forest-covered in her memory; she remembered the great trees being cut around this very site and the ground cleared. Her cousin and husband had been somewhat of a scapegrace and blackguard in England; there was some suspicion of forgery or other felony. At any rate, she had defied everyone and had married him just one day before she had sailed with him to the new country.

In the new raw country there was no elegant society, little civilization. They drifted westward and arrived in new territory, all foothills and flat wide valleys and Indians and forest. There were only a few settlers. Here, said Margot tranquilly, they would live.

The little settlement grew. Sam Hamilton took his place arrogantly among the men. He worked as hard as any of them; he plowed the rich untouched earth, made rude furniture, sowed and harvested, fought marauding Indians, smoked a big pipe. Margot bore five children in the thick-walled log cabin, buried two of them at the edge of the forest.

Her speech took on the color and rough vitality of the other settlers; her hands became gnarled, the fingernails broken. Her face was burned a rich brown, and her black eyes and straight black hair gave her the look of Indian blood. She tucked up her homespun skirts for easy striding; there was no man in the settlement taller than she.

She never forgot the night that Sam died. She had pulled him, bed and all, near to the fire, for the snow was thick on the ledges of the narrow windows, and at night they could hear the howling of the timber wolves beneath a glittering moon. She sat beside him for long hours. The dying man did not move; neither did his wife seem to move. At length she rose, took a candlestick, and went into the children's room. In that room stood her one huge ironbound box which she had brought from England. In it lay some of her old dresses, rich satins, furred cloaks, glinting brocades; her remaining pieces of jewelry, a garnet necklace and a pair of garnet earrings bordered with tiny seed pearls now discolored with age;

several old books of Shakespeare, Milton, and Ben Jonson. She drew forth a gown, all gold brocade, delicate lace rustling. She also took out her garnet jewelry and a fan of black lace stitched with tiny pearls.

Once back with Sam, she removed her homespun dress, slipped the brocade over her brawny shoulders and great brown arms. The fastenings would not meet, but she did not mind that. She hung her garnets in her ears, and about her throat she clasped the garnet necklace. She drew her hands vaguely over the rough black coils of her hair with its streaks of gray. The gown hung on her, misshapen and drawn into folds not intended by the dressmaker. Yet she had an austere dignity that would have precluded laughter. The firelight picked red points of light from the garnets, golden threads from the brocade.

Margot sat down again and took up her vigil. On the stretched brocade of her lap lay the black lace fan, its jewels glittering restlessly. She waited.

Moments crept on. A log fell heavily on the hearth and threw up a shower of golden sparks. Then Sam opened his eyes. They were filmed with approaching death.

Margot did not move. Sam stared at her heavily for a long time, as though trying to focus. Then he seemed to start; he stared more acutely. Margot sat, unmoving, the fire to the side of her, coppery and restless, gleaming in the jewels, finding shadows of light in the brocade. She was immense, majestic and ludicrous.

He continued to stare, his weary eyes traveling over her. And then of a sudden he began to laugh, helplessly, weakly, the tears starting from his eyes, rolling down his sunken cheeks. Margot still did not move, but a smile touched her mouth. She lifted the black fan; with great affectations of daintiness she fanned herself, coquetting with Sam with Gargantuan coyness. He sobbed loudly with laughter; at last he lay spent.

Margot, still smiling, knelt beside him, smoothed his grayed hair with a tender hand. He stared in her face, childishly grave, and at peace. Then he laughed a little again. His laughter rose; suddenly it congealed in a cry;

he struggled in her arms, twisted, and collapsed. Gently she lay him back on his rough pillows; gently she closed his eyes.

She had staked out one hundred acres of land. It was a terrible struggle to wrench from it sustenance for her children and for herself. During the years that followed Sam's death she became grim, harsh of hand. Her little daughter succumbed to one hideous winter; her two sons were restless unhappy boys. The eldest went still farther west with a caravan of pioneers. Two years later she heard of his death in an Indian raid. The younger boy, Oliver, remained with his mother, unhappy and savage.

Slowly the acres began to slip through Margot's hands until only twenty were left. She worked grimly, with only slight assistance from Oliver.

Many of her neighbors had long since moved into town. There were many strangers about her now, the Blodgetts, the Hobarts, the Kings, and the MacKensies. She had little to do with them. She hated the Blodgetts, who were shiftless, the Hobarts, who were upstarts, the Kings, who were crafty, the MacKensies, who were austere and insulting. When Oliver was twenty years old, he married one of Silas King's many daughters, and brought her to his mother to support. The girl was frail and shifty-eyed, and Margot literally worked her to death, in her sultry hatred. The girl died when her son, young Peter, was born. Between Margot and Oliver there was a silent inflexible hatred. One night he ran away and she never heard from him again. She brought up young Peter with grimness, and without love, at first. But the boy, she soon discovered, was like herself—sturdy, logical, strong. But she never forgave him for marrying Melinda Blodgett, another like his mother. When the friction between the old and the young woman became too great, Peter sensibly built a crude three-room shack at the other extreme end of the twenty acres, and took his bride there. Margot remained in her two-room cabin.

Peter was strong; he became a blacksmith. The twenty acres, with the exception of five cultivated by Margot, fell into decay. Melinda bore ten children; five survived, four girls and a boy. Margot loved only Margaret, the eldest daughter.

She taught Margaret to read; out of her old ironbound box, she had taken her few books. Ignorant of the world growing about her, Margaret could quote Hamlet's soliloquy faultlessly and with understanding; the tragedy of Macbeth was real to her; the tender beauty of Romeo and Juliet moved her deeply. Peter, shamefully proud of his eldest daughter, had newspapers brought to her, though he himself could neither read nor write, and boasted of it. Nevertheless, like her great-grandmother, she loved the earth. She was tall and strong and slender, brown of skin and black of eye. She was also very beautiful, and her features were delicately made.

Now, old Margot Hamilton was nearly ninety; her great-granddaughter, Margaret, or Margot, as the old woman insisted upon calling her, was nearly nineteen, a wild impulsive girl, barefooted half the year, wearing her long black hair in two swinging braids between her proud, straight shoulders. The Blodgetts and the Kings and the MacKensies sniffed at her, called her "that young savage with no refinement." The neighbors had long since dismissed the Hamilton family; they were pagans, ostracized from decent God-fearing society. Only the Blodgetts remembering their daughter Melinda was the wife of Peter, kept up a stiff and distant communication, tried to induce Peter to send his children to school. But Peter had driven them all away. The Hamilton family lived rudely and boisterously, except for Melinda, who had retreated from the unequal conflict into whining invalidism.

With stupefaction and dismay, the country folk heard of John Hobart's infatuation with Margaret Hamilton. John Hobart, the richest man in ten counties, the arbiter of the whole countryside! He could have had the finest girl in Whitmore, even in Williamsburg, the state capital. And it was now an established fact that he wished to marry Margaret Hamilton. The country folk were dumfounded.

Why, the girl ran unchecked about the countryside,

her hair down around her shoulders, her dress revealing her long legs, her hands stained brown by the sun, as nobody's should be. She had never been to school, could not sew a stitch; John Hobart's infatuation was bewildering.

But it was not bewildering to old Margot Hamilton as she watched Margaret stroke the head of her dog and look off to the brazen hills beneath the pale amber of the evening sky.

For a long time Margaret stared at the hills and scratched the head of her dog, and Margot, squatting on a tree stump in her garden, watched her. She liked to see the figure of the girl outlined darkly against the pale sky. It was strong and slender, the glistening black braids hanging between her shoulders, her vital profile lifted, the dark crimson lips parted. Margot smiled, rubbed her dry old hands together. The smile was at once compassionate and bitter.

"Margot," she called, "what are you thinking about, girl?"

Margaret started a little, turned her head. She smiled, but her eyes were vague.

"Oh, I wasn't really thinking, Granny." She began to walk toward her grandmother, the dog at her heels, her flimsy dress outlining every curve of her splendid young body. She stopped to smell a late rose, touched it with a tender finger. She stood at last before old Margot.

"I think I'd better be going along home. It's late. Want me to milk Bossy before I go, Granny?"

"No. Leave her be. I'll tend to her in a minute." She looked at the girl sharply. "You're a great lass, Margot. Well, girl, made up your mind to marry Johnny Hobart yet?"

Margot shook her head dubiously. Over her dark face a darker shadow settled. "I almost think I won't, after all, Granny. Johnny ain't got, I mean, hasn't, any real feelings."

Margot snorted contemptuously. "Sounds for all the world like that Ralph Blodgett! Thought you had better sense, Margot."

"Oh, Granny, but it's true. John hardly ever reads even a newspaper, and he just laughs at poetry. Sometimes I almost hate him when he makes fun of the things I love. He can't talk about anything but crops and cattle and building a new house, and—"

"Well, what else is there in life, you stupid child? Those are real things. The things that Blodgett boy talks about ain't living. What do you want, anyways?"

Margaret looked at the ground. Under her tanned skin there crept a crimson stain. "I want to live," she said, almost inaudibly.

"To live? What do you mean by that, Margot?" The old woman's smile was still derisive, but there was something close to pain in her eyes.

Margaret lifted her head, her manner confused.

"Why, I mean— beauty, Granny. Not just getting up at daybreak and doing the chores and working all day until you're so tired you just fall into bed at night. There must be something more than that in living. There must be men and women somewhere who think about, well—poetry—and softer things, things that last after you're dead. I want to be like them. I guess I can't explain it very clearly."

The old woman slowly got to her feet, her stiff knees creaking. She grasped her gnarled stick with one hand, with the other she touched Margot's elbow imperatively. "Come with me," she said. She began to hobble out of the flower garden, and Margaret, frowning, followed her. They progressed slowly over the broken ground to the edge of a clump of old trees on the other side of the cabin and sat down on a fallen trunk. For a long time old Margot stared before her. Six paces away, there were four slightly sunken places in the earth. She pointed to them with her stick.

"There lie my husband and my three children," she said. Margaret stared and shivered a little.

"You remember what we read in Macbeth, Margot? 'Life is a tale, told by an idiot, full of sounds and fury, signifying nothing?' Remember that. Look at them graves. They prove it, Margot. What do you and that soft boy cousin of yours talk about? I know. You told me once. Souls and hereafters and meaning of life, and whether there is a God, or something, and how mystifying and hopeless things are, in general. I 'spect, at times, he even talks about life not being worth the living. Perhaps it is. Perhaps it ain't. I don't know anything, Margot, and I've lived a good sight of years. Only fools and very young folks think they know what life's all about. But now that I'm old, there's only one real thing to me, lass. This."

She stooped, bending her head between her ancient knees, and scooped up a clod of earth. She held it before Margaret's eyes.

"This, lass. Earth. That's the only real thing. Earth." She touched the girl's forehead with a broken fingertip. "And there's the enemy, lass. In there. Full of sickness and self-deceit. Oh, it's a grand thing when that enemy talks, and puts God in his place, and the world and men! Makes the owner think he's a sort of little god himself, proud of his misery. Nothing seems to have substance to him. And after a while, he comes to believe the enemy in his head, his brain, and life retreats from him, lass. Then he dies. After that, what? This. This piece of earth, at last. The only reality gets him when the enemy's mouth is closed with death."

Margaret still said nothing. She averted her head.

"I've lived ninety years, lass. And I still don't know any more about it than that dog there. Yet young fools like Ralph Blodgett always know, talking about the final reality."

Margaret looked at her sullenly. "But, Shakespeare talked so, and so did Milton and Voltaire—"

"Yes, they did. But they had health in them. There's no health in that Ralph Blodgett. Not yet, anyway. I ain't saying a man can't look for God and wonder about everything, so long as he keeps his feet firm in the earth. These men did. They were men of the earth, strong and steady, and they could afford to listen to the enemy in their heads occasionally. But this Blodgett boy; he has no feeling for the land, no strength. He thinks to work until you sweat is vulgar. Thinks his boredom sets him apart, makes him better than real folks. But his boredom, if it is real, is only proof of a blank spirit."

"You mean you want me to marry John Hobart, is that it, Granny?"

Margot slowly let the clod of earth fall.

"You've got to decide that yourself, Margot. But with Johnny Hobart, rascal that he is, you'll be safe. Safe from Ralph's things that will destroy you, make you sick, and in the end make you wish you'd never set eyes on him. He—"

"Oh, Granny, you make me tired! He's a poet, a real poet! And someday the world will recognize that—"

"I shouldn't wonder," said the old woman with a shrug. "The world always recognizes fools, especially fools that despise it."

The girl stood up as though she could endure hearing no more. She started to speak, and then with a fierce gesture she strode off, her dog following her with more spirit now that they were homeward bound. Margot watched her tall strong figure striding over the meadow until the evening dimness made it unreal. The hills were quite dark now, gloomy and colorless. Distant cattle were lowing; in the barn behind the cabin old Bossy stamped, demanding.

"I'll go milk you soon, drat you!" muttered the old woman.

She leaned back against the trunk of the tree, looked over the land, lifted her eyes to the sky.

"I don't know," she muttered again. "I don't know." She felt very tired. She closed her eyes. Her shapeless garments, her powerful old figure, were absorbed in the dimness that overtook the woods. Soon she was not distinguishable from the other shadows about her.

At the other side of the valley, a pale moon drifted over the crest of the hills behind which the sun had so recently sunk. It began to outline the dark hulk of the mountains in ghostly light. Margot still sat, leaning against the trunk of the tree. Her eyes were closed, her great old arms on her knees, part of the clod of earth still between her fingers.

All night long the distant farmers heard the distressed lowing and crying of old Bossy. Once or twice a dog howled, and some superstitious farm woman shivered in her warm bed and murmured that there would be death that night.

Chapter Three

Margaret, STRIDING RAPIDLY over the fields as though running from something, was also muttering to herself, "I don't know. My God, I don't know!"

She circled a clump of whispering trees, whose shadow was beginning to be faintly outlined on the brown earth. She came in sight of the three-room shack where she lived. Margaret suddenly thought of Ralph's cold derision when he mentioned her home. She was filled with mingled resentment against him, and also a sadness.

She remembered what old Margot had said once: "We strong ones are always drawn to weaker men. I don't know why. Perhaps it's because nature intended us to breed them out. But seems as like they destroy us before we can do much about it. They eat us up."

She was near the house now. It stood, stark and alone, as though a group of maples nearby had withdrawn from it fastidiously. It leaned, its clapboards gray and broken under the moon. The windows were uncurtained. Behind the house loomed the outbuildings, dark and untidy.

She pushed open the kitchen door and her ears were assaulted by familiar quarreling voices. The wooden floor was stained with dirt and grease, and uncovered. The walls were of knotted pine; on one wall was an iron bracket in which smoldered a dirty oil lamp. On the table stood another lamp, reeking of coal oil. In one corner of the room fumed an ancient wood stove, littered with scraps of burned food. In a woodbox near the stove, the wood was covered with eggshells, scraps, and the scrapings of Peter's pipe.

It was hot in the kitchen, and very noisy. The children, as usual, were squabbling among themselves. At intervals Peter would reach across the littered table and smite one of his ragged offspring, who would scream. Beyond the table, in a corner, stood a "pallet," on which Margaret and Linda slept, the fraying quilts sweeping the dust of the floor. Behind the table stood Bobbie, six years old; it was his turn tonight to wave a "branch" over the heads of the family to keep off the flies.

Melinda Hamilton sat across the table, with its litter of salt pork and beans and jugs of molasses, opposite her husband. She was a thin woman with gray hair, pale blue eyes, and a long horselike face. She had once been pretty, but there was no sign of it now.

Peter ate like a wolf, his powerful shoulders hunched forward over the table; he shoveled food into his great mouth with a fork or a knife or anything handy. His dark blue shirt was splotched with sweat.

The family did not look up, with the exception of Peter, when Margaret entered slowly, the lamplight shining on her black braids. Peter frowned at her but could not be entirely displeased. The sloping neckline of her dress revealed the strong brown neck.

"Where you been?" he barked. "Traipsin' around with the ole woman, I bet. Gassin' for hours, doin' nothin'. And all the pertatoes not in yet, and the grapes—"

"Leave me be," snapped Margaret. Unconsciously she reverted to his own manner of speech. "I worked every blessed hour from sunup to sundown, like I always do, and then you raise the devil if I run off a minute." She pushed a chair between her father's and Linda's, and, snatching a tin plate, she filled it with food.

"Ain't been nobody here a minute today to give a body a drink of water," her mother complained. "Lands sakes, a body might as well be dead as a burden on her folks. Seems like, though, with a pack of young uns, and one of 'em a great girl like you, Maggie, I oughtn't be left alone to git along best I can."

"Can't be two places at once," Margaret said sullenly. "Can't be a plow horse and a hired gal, too."

"You work turrible hard, don't you?" said Peter sarcastically. "Worn to the bone, poor critter. How's the ole woman? Ain't seen her in a month or more."

"She's all right," said Margaret briefly. She ate steadily. Her father's sharp eye saw the somberness of her face. He frowned.

"The ole woman ain't been settin' you agin John Hobart, be she?"

Margaret snorted. "All she been talking about today was telling me I should marry him."

Peter cocked a bushy eyebrow. "Must be changin' her tune," he ruminated. "Last time she mentioned him, she said he was nothin' but a stud horse. Hated his guts, she did. Funny."

Margaret did not reply. Suddenly the group around the table became intolerable to her, ugly and dirty beyond endurance.

"Ought to run over and see the old girl," Peter continued thoughtfully. "Thought she looked a mite poorly the last time I seen her. Ninety years old. Well, the old uns lived longer than we'll live. Good stock in 'em. I'll amble over there tomorrow."

Margaret shrugged. She stood up and began to stack the dirty dishes.

"Here, Mag, forgot to tell you John's comin' over to see you tonight. Better hurry up."

Margaret paused a moment. "Got to go out a minute or two," she muttered. Her dark face had colored painfully. "I'll be back."

Peter ceased stuffing his pipe and glowered.

"Runnin' out to chase over the country with that good-for-nothin' Ralph again, eh?" he roared. "No, you ain't, my gal. That's got to stop, and it's stoppin' right now! Even Johnny Hobart's heard about it. It ain't decent, and you're big enough now to know it."

Margaret faced him. Her fists clenched themselves fiercely.

"Leave Ralph Blodgett be!" she shouted. "I'll tend to him. I don't need no help from anyone. He—he ain't what you think he is, Pa. He's a genius!"

Peter narrowed his eyes.

"Now, what may a genius be?" he drawled. "Does it chop wood and shoe horses and bring home the bacon for the woman to cook? Or does it just sit and star gaze, bein' soulful and too good for ord'nry folks? If that's what it is, I don't want no hide nor hair of it around here," he added in a suddenly harsh tone. "Now, git to work, and be ready to see John when he comes. And mind what you say to him, my gal, or it'll be the worse for you."

Margaret faced him without fear, though her lips whitened. "I'm agoin' to see Ralph for a minute," she said quietly. "If you don't let me go, I won't see John tonight, and I won't say to him what I 'tended to say."

For a moment the eyes of father and daughter locked. Then Peter softened. So, the gal was goin' to be sensible, prob'ly goin' to tell that young squirt that she was agoin' to marry John Hobart. He grinned.

"Well, go on, then. But, mind you," he added warningly, "you be back right quick, or I'll come after you with a stick."

In a moment Margaret had vanished through the door into the darkness beyond. In the kitchen, flies settled thickly over the remnants of the meal. Melinda rubbed her nose. She was secretly gratified. If Maggie'd come to her senses, then there'd allus be enough vittles in the larder. She hated her daughter, wanted her out of the house, and wanted to profit by her going. She secretly hoped John would beat her frequently.

Margaret ran swiftly over the dark earth. Her shawl floated about her shoulders, her braids streamed behind her. Soon the house, with its rawly lit windows, was far behind. In the distance she saw a clump of dark trees, their crests whitened by the moon, their shadows thick on the ground. As she came up to them, a tall slender young man emerged from the gloom, spoke her name. She caught at his hand, pulled him along.

"Come on," she panted. "Let's go up the hill to our place!"

She ran on. He followed her, but she ran more easily and soon the distance between them widened. Her shadow streaked behind her, grotesque and wavering and leaping.

She reached the top of the hill, stood outlined against the sky, watching the ascent of her cousin. She might have been a dark statue, remote and somber.

When Ralph came up to her, she touched his arm and murmured tensely, "I have something to tell you. Sit down here, beside me."

He sat down, uneasy, and rested his elbows on his knees, staring down into the valley.

He was a tall wiry youth, but somehow he gave the impression of delicacy. He had long, thin, well-shaped hands, so different, Margaret always thought, from the blunt fingers of the other men she knew. His nose was his best feature, thin and straight, and almost noble. His eyes were blue and he had a shock of fine light hair which glistened in the moonlight. He gave an impression of mingled shyness and arrogance.

"Well, what is it?" he demanded, in the light voice that had always seemed so musical to Margaret. Now, for some reason, she found it exasperating.

She drew a deep and shaken breath. "I was talking to Granny today," she began, and then was suddenly unable to go on.

"Well?"

Margaret was silent. He could not see the tears on her face.

Ralph shrugged. There was a real storm in him tonight. He, too, had something to say. He was going away to Williamsburg, perhaps even to New York. He could stay here no longer; he was smothering in this atmosphere. He had been sent by his mother through all the schools in Whitmore. Margaret had lent him old Margot's books; they had spent hours whispering over them on this same hilltop. Now he must go away. But, he had decided, Margaret would go with him. He had some money wheedled from his doting mother. He would take his scribbled mounds of poems with him; somewhere in that bright and shimmering world were men who awaited his message!

Ralph sighed; he could not summon interest in anything Margaret had to say tonight. He was elated at the thought of departure, finally, but he was sick, a little sick at the thought of anyone but Margaret reading his poems. He had instinctive taste, and deep within him he knew his gifts were second-rate. It was a thought he could not face too often, for without poetry he was naked.

He looked at the stars thrusting their points through the pale sky; he looked at the moon, remote and terrible.

"Margaret," he sighed. "Sometimes I'm so afraid. Sometimes I feel so strong that nothing, nobody, could hurt me, and the next minute it's all blank, empty. I can't seem to rouse myself. If only I could *feel*, Margaret. Feel something in myself that was hard and purposeful. But there is nothing, nothing even to live for."

Margaret had heard variations of this hundreds of times. But tonight, she could only see old Margot sitting on the dead log, the coppery sunlight on every seam of her face, her knees spread, yet strong, the clod of living earth in her hands. The vision was so strong that she could have sworn that she saw her grandmother's very face.

She felt a sudden hatred. She wanted to shout at him, "Look at the earth, you fool! Feel it in your hands, the good warm earth! Look down there, where people are sleeping, after a day's work and a day's sweat, happy to be able to sleep, happy to wake up tomorrow, and push their feet in the earth again! That's where reality is, that's where life is!"

So intense were her thoughts that she stood up abruptly, full of exultance. Ralph stared up at her in amazement.

"You're not going yet, Margaret?" he said. "I've got lots of things I want to talk over with you."

He waited for her to sit down again, looking up expectantly. But she would not. She could not endure him tonight; she felt that she despised him. Then she was flooded with compassion for him, and tenderness overwhelmed her. She bent quickly and touched his forehead with her lips. He clung to her suddenly; her spirit bent back from him desperately, holding onto the color of reality. Involuntarily her body straightened, and he rose to his feet, still clinging to her. They stared at each other in the moonlight; its pale glimmer shone in Margaret's face. Her eyes were on fire, filled with living brilliance; her face glowed with an inner vitality. Never had she been so beautiful. The young man was dazzled.

"Oh, Maggie, darling!" he cried. "I love you so!"

He put his arms around her, kissed her neck.

In her tenderness she let him hold her. She smoothed his hair with her brown young fingers.

He was whispering, "Maggie, I'm going away in a few weeks. Far away. To give the world what I can give it. And you must come with me. We'll be married, as we have always intended." He kissed her warm neck again.

There were tears in her black eyes; she looked over his head at the quiet night sky. She felt very close to God, humble, yet full of exquisite happiness.

"I must go now," she said softly. She had already left him. She slipped from his arms and began to run, like a shadow. He called after her; she did not turn, did not look back. She felt that she was running back to life.

Chapter Four

At intervals Peter went to the door and listened for Margaret's return. There was no sound. He shut the door savagely and stood gnawing his lip. Melinda smirked.

"Wal, it's more'n an hour, and she ain't back!" she gloated.

"Shut up," growled Peter. But his tone was absent-minded; he spoke merely from habit. He clenched his mighty fists. "By God, I'll break her back!"

"Time you did," sniffed his wife.

There was a curt knock; Peter pulled the door open. John Hobart stood outside, a forced expression of amiability on his face.

"Howdy," he said and entered the kitchen. "Howdy, Mis' Hamilton."

He turned to Peter. "Where's Maggie? I ain't got but a little while and I want to see her."

Peter, though his eyes were angry, welcomed the visitor with a grin.

"Here, set a while, John. Come on in the settin' room, and wait a minute—"

"Say, ain't Maggie here?" John's voice became suddenly ominous.

"Sure she is! Just step' out a minute. Back right away."

"Runnin' around with that fool again, eh? Well, damn it, she can—" John turned; he would have left the room in a towering rage, but Margaret's face rose before him again. If he left now, he would never see her again. He turned back to Peter; his face was black.

"I'll wait," he said shortly. "No, I'll go find her, myself. She can't be far, you say."

"Better let me go, John."

"No, I'll go myself. And depends on what I find whether I come back or not."

He slammed the door after him and strode off, full of hatred, and as he went, he looked across the moonlit valley. Was it his imagination, or did he really see a running shadow across the flatness? Yes, there it was again, just emerging from the gloom of a clump of trees. It was running lightly and swiftly. It was Margaret, running back to him! Instantly something frightful in him relaxed.

He began to run toward the girl, calling to her. Hearing his voice, Peter opened the kitchen door, stood watching. He saw John's figure meet Margaret's; he saw the two figures dissolve into one. There was silence, broken only by the night wind in the dying trees, the distant lowing of a forgotten cow in distress. Smiling in vast relief, Peter shut the door and stood rubbing his hands.

After that involuntary embrace, Margaret withdrew herself gently from John's arms. Laughing shakenly, she looked up at his vital face. It was almost gentle, filled with an unbelieving happiness. Her hands slipped along his arms, feeling the strength and power of him. She felt a little sorry for him; she did not love him, but at his touch something that had little to do with love set her afire, made her legs as weak as water. It was very confusing.

He put his arm about her, and in a sudden silence they began to walk slowly toward the hills she had just left.

I don't love him! thought Margaret. I really love Ralph. But even this, to her increasing amazement, did not make her wish to return to Ralph. In the clasp of John's arm she felt peace. When he bent and kissed her lips, it seemed to her that she was engulfed in languid flame, and her trembling was renewed.

They came to a gentle hollow between two hills and sat down. John took Margaret's hands; he kissed the palms, slowly and lingeringly. She tried to speak, to break the spell that was subduing her, but she could not. She thought that she must die in the access of her delicious surrender. Ralph was not forgotten; but she knew that he had nothing to do with this. Never had he aroused one quicker pulse in her body.

John's lips had moved from her hands to her throat; she could endure no more and she gently pushed him from her. When she spoke her voice was slightly hoarse.

"Was I late?"

"Sure, very late," he murmured, pushing aside her hands and kissing the hollow in her throat. But Margaret still fought against the insidious urge to surrender. She drew away a little.

"You want me to marry you, don't you, John? Well, I'm ready to marry you if you want me."

"Want you!" The man's voice was guttural. "You damn well know I do! God, you're a witch! I couldn't live without you. I'd—I'd kill another man if he so much as looked at you!"

He grasped her again; under the hot pressure of his mouth her will dissolved, but, strangely, Ralph's face stood between hers and John's. She wrenched herself from him.

"What's the matter?" he grunted. "Don't tell me you don't like it!"

"I do," she replied without shame. "I don't know why it is! But listen, John. I've got to tell you something. Will you please listen? Well, then, Ralph asked me to marry him and go away with him. I— I'm sorry for Ralph; folks hereabouts never understood him. Please, don't say anything just yet. I've got to tell you. He's going away; he thinks I—love him. He's got to go away thinking that; he's not to know about us, John. If he knows about it, he'll never have a chance where he's going. And it's important to me that he has a chance. So, let's not tell anyone just yet, John. I'll tell Pa, that's all. You won't mind if I say you want it that way?"

"See here!" he cried angrily. "How long's that young pup goin' to hang around here, anyways? I'm not a piece of dead meat, Mag."

"From what he said, he'll be leaving soon; probably not more than three-four weeks."

"And you expect me to wait all that time, when I was planning for us to be married in a couple days?"

"You've waited a long time. You can wait a little

longer." She smiled to herself in the darkness; it thrilled her to be so desired. "Besides, you know how folks talk when a wedding's too quick!" And she laughed.

At the implication in her laughter, his blood rose again. He seized her; she could not even struggle in that iron grip. He bore her down, his breath hot in her face. She closed her eyes; her repelling hands relaxed on his shoulders.

"Well, I've got somethin' comin', if I let you do that!" he whispered fiercely in her ear. She made no reply; she could not. Her surrender was complete.

After a long time they began to talk again. Upon drinking from a long withheld pitcher, a man's thirst is finally slaked. But, strangely, John's thirst was not slaked by the drinking. He had thought that could he but possess Margaret Hamilton once, his desire for her would pass. But, as though he had drunk salt water, his thirst mounted. She belonged to him; nothing under God's sky would take her from him now.

They lay side by side in each other's arms. And it was also strange that Margaret believed that now she did not love him one jot the more; he had not touched what Ralph called "the inner spirit." She was still inviolate in the hidden places of herself. Nevertheless, her desire for John was not satisfied, would never be satisfied.

They slept, side by side, even as their lips met again. They had not been conscious of the sustained lowing of the distressed cow, though its lamentations had been a background to everything that had transpired.

The cool gray dawn was drifting foggily through the trees when Margaret awoke. For a moment she did not know where she was. Her eyes blinked at the dim black tracery of the trees against the paling sky.

She sat up; John still slept beside her, one arm flung across her body. The air was very cold. She could see across the valley, could see the mist coiling over the ground.

For a moment she was held by this hushed silence; then she shook John, laughed, kissed him to confused and grunting consciousness.

"Look—we've slept here all night! Pa'll kill me."

"Let him touch one hair of your head and I'll break his back," said John. "Here, kiss me."

The kiss was as ardent as the first, and for a long moment they embraced. They then scrambled to their feet; Margaret was filled with joy and a deep contentment.

Suddenly she lifted her head, drew her clear black brows together, and listened. She recognized distress calls in an animal.

"Seems to me I heard that cow all night," she murmured. She turned in the direction of the sound. "Sounds like Granny's old Bossy," she continued uneasily. "Let's go over there and see what's the matter. Let's tell her that we are going to be married. She's always up at dawn."

She ran ahead, uneasiness pricking at her more acutely every moment. John followed; his heavier step could hardly keep up with hers. They came in sight of the little cabin on its slight rise of ground. It was desolate, sharply defined now against the brightening rose of the sky. Chickens were clucking raucously for release.

Margaret ran to the door, thrust it open, called. There was no answer. She called again, in so loud and frightened a voice that John involuntarily said, "Hush." She went into the cabin, still calling. A moment later she came out; her face was pale.

"She's not there!"

Margaret stood in the garden, tense and silent, but her eyes darted everywhere. Then she gave a cry and pointed a trembling finger to the edge of the trees at the bottom of the garden.

John followed the pointing of her finger. In the thinning shadow of the trees they could see old Margot sitting, her head on her breast, her knees spraddled, her hands hanging between them, lifelessly. Margaret, weeping loudly, ran toward the figure. She felt a strong clutch on her arm, and, so suddenly impeded in progress, she whirled staggeringly on her heel.

John had seen in the attitude of the old woman something that he did not want Margaret to see without preparation.

"Maggie, dear, I want to tell you something," he said. "The old woman—dead. Margaret—I think she's dead. I kin see it from here. Better let me go first."

Margaret began to sob weakly. He put his arm about her. Together they went to old Margot. The dawn wind fluttered her slack garments; the dawn light lay on her dead and open eyes. In her fingers remained a small lump of earth.

"Oh, Granny," said Margaret, and then could say no more. John patted her shoulder.

"Maggie," he said, "that cow's sufferin' some. Suppose you go 'tend to her, and I'll do what's got to be done for the ole woman. Run along now, like a good girl."

Sobbing, her head bent, Margaret went into the ancient barn. The cow was stamping, tossing her tortured head, her eyes glaring in the gloom. Margaret forced herself to make a comforting sound. The tears were running down her cheeks; she could hardly see. She found the stool, picked up a bucket, and sat down beside the miserable animal who looked at her gratefully. Bossy nuzzled her softly.

Margaret carried out the milk and poured it into the chicken trough. She carried water into the barn for the cow. Mechanically, she fed the animal. When this was done, she went toward the cabin again. Old Margot had disappeared.

The door stood open; she entered, her feet heavy. She found John standing beside old Margot. He had laid her upon her rude maple bed and had closed her eyes and crossed her hands on her breast. He looked up as Margaret entered, put his arm about her.

"Well, that's all, I 'spect," he said heavily. He had known the old woman well. She had driven him repeatedly from her tiny apple orchard when he had been a boy, brandishing her cane. They had hated each cordially, but they had respected each other.

Margaret bent over her grandmother, tears dropping onto the dead face.

"Granny," she whispered. "God bless you, Granny. It's all right, now."

She kissed the cold forehead, then without looking at John, she went out again into the morning. He left her alone a while, then followed her. She was looking at the hills. Tears still poured over her cheeks, but her face was calm.

Finally she went to the barn and led out old Bossy.

"I'm taking her home," she said.

"I'll go with you," answered John. They walked slowly and in silence across the damp fields. Before they reached Margaret's home, Peter ran out to meet them. His face was black with rage. He glanced at Margaret with such scorn that she flinched, but his business was with John. He brandished his fist in the younger man's face.

"So that's how you want my gal, is it?" he shouted. "Keepin' her out all night doin' God knows what, except you know! And I know, too! By God, I'll slit your throat for this!"

John caught his wrist, twisted it, and then pushed Peter from him with a contemptuous gesture.

Margaret got between the two men. Her father raised his fist and smashed it into her face. She staggered, felt blood pouring from her mouth and nose. She sank down to the ground on her hands and knees.

Dimly she heard roars, shouts, thuds. She could not see yet. She felt herself lifted, felt a gentle hand wiping the blood from her eyes.

"All right, Maggie?" asked John in a thickened voice. "I'll kill him for this, by God, I will!" he added through his teeth.

Peter was lying sprawled on his back in the stubble. He was slowly raising his head; tentatively he felt his mangled jaw. John left Margaret, seized Peter by the front of his shirt, dragged him to his feet. He caught the older man close to him, thrust his face into the dazed face of the other. There was murder in his eyes.

"Lay your hand on my gal agin, Peter Hamilton, and I'll tear you into sausage meat," he growled, shaking the battered man fiercely. "Listen, you pore fool: your ole Granny is dead. Mag and me heard her ole cow bawling last night and went over to see what was the trouble. The ole woman was dying. We stayed all night; she died a little while ago. Damn you, does that satisfy you?"

Melinda, in a shawl, fluttered from the house like a scarecrow figure. Her eyes darted to Margaret, and seeing the bruised face of the girl, she could not refrain from a venomous smirk. She turned on John like a weak fury, trying to loosen his hands from Peter's neck.

"You leave him be!" she shrieked. "You leave him be, Johnny Hobart! Get out off our land, and take that shameless gal with ye! We don't want you here!"

John looked down into her malignant eyes and flung Peter from him. Peter staggered, got his balance, thrust his wailing wife aside. He spoke to her, but his face was turned to John. He tried to grin.

"Shut up, Melindy. I was all wrong about this here business. Everythin's all right. I just sort of lost my temper. John and Maggie spent the night with the ole woman. An' she died this morning."

He advanced upon the lowering John, extending his hand frankly.

"Here, now, no hard feelin's, John? You can hit like a mule, and no lyin', either. Shouldn't have lost my temper. Wal, you're the better man."

John glowered; he stiffly allowed his hand to be shaken. Peter's good nature was entirely restored. He did not look at Margaret; he was ashamed to do so.

"That's all very well!" said John grimly. "But, damn you, lay your hand on my gal again and you'll never touch her another time! That clear? We're goin' to be married soon, so shut up! Take her home with you; then you better see 'bout buryin' the ole woman!"

He turned to Margaret, took her in his arms. Despite the shock of her father's blow, she smiled with delighted amusement up into his face. He kissed her with a hard, short kiss, then walked to his horse, still tethered near the house. He swung himself into the saddle and rode away without a backward glance.

"Wal!" shrilled Melinda. "I don't know what this is all about, but seems like you made a fool of yourself, as usual, Pete Hamilton! Allus flyin' off the handle 'bout nothin' an' gettin' yourself in trouble. An' then makin' our gal the talk of the country, bangin' her 'round and makin' out like she was a bad woman!" She turned to Margaret. "He sure banged you up, didn't he, Maggie? Come on home, Maggie, and we'll wash you up."

Maggie smiled a little to herself. She led old Bossy up to her father demurely, dropped the rope before him, and then walked away with her mother.

Peter looked after them. Suddenly he shouted with laughter.

Chapter Five

THEY did not bury old Margaret in the neat country graveyard which huddled about the Baptist Church.

Margaret and her mother had opened the ironbound box in the bedroom in search of suitable garments in which to bury the old woman. The first thing they saw was a sheet of paper, written in pencil, on top of all the other things. It was dated a year ago.

"When I die (it read) I want to be buried in my old gold brocade wrapped in newspaper at the bottom of this box. I want my gold kid slippers on my feet. And I want to be buried near my husband, Sam Hamilton, and my children. To my great-granddaughter, Margaret Hamilton, I leave my land, everything upon it, and everything she can find in my cabin. I also want her to have all my books, and my garnet earrings and garnet necklace, which I want her to wear when she marries Johnny Hobart. I leave nothing to anyone else."

This odd will was signed carefully: "Margot Hamilton, May 19, 1871, Whitmore township, Wayne County."

So old Margot was laid beside the sunken grave of her husband. The country folk were scandalized. To be buried like this, in unsanctified ground, like a heathen! No minister, either, no flowers, no mourning!

No one came to the funeral, for no one was invited. Peter Hamilton dug the grave himself. The coffin was of plain pine, ungarnished. Old Margot was carefully put into her old gold brocade.

The ironbound box was removed, the chickens carried to the Hamilton barn. Everything else was left as old Margot had left it. Peter nailed the cabin door shut. The Hamiltons went home in a copper sunset glow, in unaccustomed silence.

Margaret looked over the contents of the box. Ancient dresses, most of them moldering. But there was one, made of yards and yards of ivory silk, embroidered with huge splashes of bright red roses and green leaves. It had a tight bodice, cut very low, the neck a mass of ruffles made of spidery French lace. From it emanated a strange fragrance, musty yet haunting. Margaret held its silken coolness to her cheek.

"I'll be married in this!" she whispered. "Ma can make it over a little. You beautiful thing!"

She held up the garnet earrings and necklace, and caught the sunlight in the ruddy jewels and small pale pearls. She put away her treasures carefully after removing the books, locked the box, and hung the key about her neck.

It was Sunday. The smaller children were out playing in the fields; Melinda drowsed in the bare bedroom she shared with her husband. Margaret sat on the edge of the stoop. In an hour she and her mother were going to drive over to see Susie, Ralph's mother, if Peter had returned, by then, in the buggy.

Margaret's thoughts were dark. When she was away from John, she thought of him with indifference and even distaste, shot through with a sense of guilty excitement. She remembered then how brutal were his hands, how empty of subtlety was his ruddy face. She considered her future life with him. They would live in the fine new stone house he was going to build; they would have children; there would be large acres to watch yield, neighbors who would visit; and then—? Nothing. No one to talk to, not even Granny.

The splintered wood of the stoop was warm under her fingers; she ran her hand distractedly over it. A warm drop fell on the back of her hand.

"Oh, I don't love him; I don't! Ralph, I love you. I'll always love you," she whispered.

An intense desire to see Ralph came over her. She ran into the hot dimness of the little house and knocked on her mother's door.

"Ma! Are you awake? Can't we go over to Aunt Susie's

now? It ain't far; we can walk it in half an hour. Maybe
Pa won't be back until evenin'."

Melinda's petulant voice came through the sagging
door. "Eh, Why'd you wake me up, Maggie? Go to
Susie's? No, I ain't goin' to traipse over the hills in this
heat 'out the buggy. Go on yourself; I'll have Pa drive me
over if he comes. Now, go 'way and leave me to a minute's
peace!"

Feverishly Margaret dragged an old wooden box from
beneath the bed she shared with Linda. It contained all
her wearing apparel. She pulled out a pink and green
gingham dress, white cotton stockings, and her only pair
of feminine black slippers. She dressed in trembling haste;
it had just occurred to her that John would probably be
over; she wanted to avoid him now. She tore a comb
through her thick black hair and wound it up at the
nape of her neck so that it clustered like huge black ap-
ples against her skin. She pulled a pink gingham sunbonnet over her head and ran out of the house, already
frantic with haste and heat. Dressed thus, in ordinary
clothes, she seemed somewhat awkward; her natural dignity and proud carriage were eclipsed.

She climbed the hill, panting under a sky that seemed
pale and swimming in heat. She stopped for breath at
the top of the hill and pulled off her bonnet, turning up
her face to the cool breeze. Her hair was already loosened
into shining coils on her neck, and her slippers were
white with dust.

She turned and went down the opposite side of the hill.

Susan Blodgett, her son, and her hired man, lived in
the narrow valley on the other side of the hill. Margaret
could see her aunt's house staring up at her. It was a lean,
tall, light-gray house, rambling and shabby. The early
autumn sun shone on the broken and discolored roof so
that it burned with a tawny light.

Mrs. Blodgett was lucky in her hired man, Silas Rowe,
a surly, taciturn bachelor of middle age; it was he who
had painted the white picket fence about the house and
it was he kept the grounds trim and neat. Ralph did
little, if anything. It was also Silas Rowe whose labor

furnished the Blodgett table amply. He bullied both the "widder woman" and her son; he was the tyrant of the household, and neither mother nor son dared oppose him.

Margaret was consumed with a passion of desire to see Ralph's face, to hear him speak, to wander aimlessly about the little valley with him, to touch his hand. The desire deepened into pain; there were stinging tears in her eyes as she reached the floor of the valley and hurried toward the house.

It seemed to Margaret that the very beating of her aching heart could be heard audibly in the silence. She might have been entirely alone in the world. So it was that the voices that came from the "settin' room" at the front of the house were quite audible. She stopped a moment, disappointed. Now she could see that three buggies were hitched to the poles of the stoop.

"Well," Margaret heard Susan Blodgett say. "Well, I hope you folks don't blame me for the heathen ways of them Hamiltons. T'ain't poor Melindy's fault, though her daughter Maggie is a grown girl runnin' wild like an Indian over the country with the Lord knows who!"

There was an assenting murmur of voices at this, then "old Mis' MacKensie's" voice rose shrill and sharp, "Wal, still, Susie, you ought to've said something to Melindy 'bout the way they buried the ole Granny. Land, it was scandalous! No minister, no funeral, no nothin'. 'Tain't civilized; 'tain't Christian. I heered no other folks was there but the family, and Pete Hamilton dug the grave hisself. He ought to be horsewhipped."

"But what about this girl, Margaret, you speak of, Mrs. Blodgett?" asked another voice. Margaret, who had been listening with a broad and enjoying smile, started a little, leaned forward to hear more distinctly. She had never heard this voice before; it was young and clear, and had foreign intonations.

"That's Pete Hamilton's oldest gal," replied Mrs. Mac-Kensie with a loud snort. "A strange one. Pete don't send his young 'uns to school, but they do say this gal can read and write some. But that's all she can do; brown as an Indian, with big wild eyes and long plaits, and tall and broad in the shoulders like a man. Some folks say she's a beauty, but I never seed it. Disgrace to the whole country. Runs crazy over them hills, whoopin'. If you stay till October, Lydia, you'll see her yourself."

"You won't miss much, Miss Lydia, if you don't!" chortled Susan. The others laughed stridently.

"She must be quite a character," said Miss Lydia. "I really must see her; it will amuse my friends in Williamsburg so much when I tell them about her."

"An' Johnny Hobart chasin' her like a sick calf!" exclaimed another voice, belonging to a woman whom Margaret knew as Mis' King. "Don't hear so much about it lately, though."

"Must be comin' to his senses," said Mrs. Holbrooks in a smug and disapproving voice. " 'Bout time."

"You don't mean Squire Hobart, John Hobart?" cried Miss Lydia. "You don't mean him, do you, Auntie? John Hobart? Why, you know he comes to Williamsburg three or four times a year. I've met him often; he's a wonderful man, so real and interesting! Mary Campbell's father buys most of his stock, and it was Mary's birthday, and he came. He seemed right glad to see me; danced three waltzes with me. Mary said he had a case on me, but I don't believe it! I asked him why he never called on Papa and Mamma, and he said to me, 'Do you want me to come, Miss Lydia?' And land! My face got so hot! Mary said I blushed like a whole garden of roses, but she always did exaggerate. And so I said, 'Yes, of course I do,' and he said, 'I'll come the next time.' Mary joked with him about him being a bachelor, and he looked at me so strangely and said, 'The right girl could change that.' And Mary just shrieked that I got redder and redder. Oh, I do like him a lot, and I do hope I'll see him before I go home again!"

Margaret, still listening, was conscious of a cold sensation in her breast.

"John Hobart," mused Lydia softly. "He's awful rich, isn't he, Auntie?"

"Richest man hereabouts; richer than even Mayor

Bailey in Whitmore. Could be mayor of Whitmore his-self if he wanted to," replied Mrs. Holbrooks.

"I like rich men," said Lydia in a childishly laughing voice. The others laughed fondly.

"You could do worse than Johnny Hobart," said her aunt stolidly. "Don't think no worse of him, Lydia, 'cause of that Maggie Hamilton. Men will be men, you know," she added delicately, "and bein's the Lord made them that way, we wimin folks must shut our eyes some-times and pretend like we don't see nothin'."

"What a terrible creature she must be!" said Lydia in awed tones.

Margaret felt a stiff smile lift the corners of her cold lips. She felt numb all over. Ralph was forgotten. She put up her hand against the hot side of the house to steady herself. Illuminated by flame, she saw herself and John in the gentle hollow under the dark trees that night a week ago; for the first time a sickening sensation of guilt struck her. It was not at the act itself that she stood appalled; she was appalled because she had given truth to these creatures' hints and suspicions. She had voluntarily stepped under their feet that they might trample upon her and she was in their power. All at once she wanted to descend upon them, to strike them with powerful fists.

"Wal, there ain't so much talk anyways 'bout John marryin' her, like there was," reminded Mrs. King. "My Ezra said that he heard in town yesterday that John had just ordered new fixin's and things, and loads of stone. Must be goin' to build that new house he allus talked about. Don't look like Maggie Hamilton's goin' to be the one to live in it! How about you, Miss Lydia?"

Lydia laughed softly and self-consciously. As though she were in the room, Margaret could see the teasing eyes of the ladies fixed upon the girl. She drew a deep breath, put on her bonnet again, and retreated from the house. Then she began to sing loudly, making a great noise as she approached the house again.

She stepped onto the stoop, humming. The door of the house stood open. All was dimness within, but she could distinguish in the gloom figures of the various ladies sitting about the cold fireplace. Their faces, as they turned them to her, were merely white blotches to her sun-dazzled eyes. She saw that they were drinking coffee and eating cake.

"Oh, it's you, Maggie!" exclaimed Mrs. Blodgett in a falsely affectionate voice. Her eyes shifted from the girl. "We were just settin' here out of the heat, where it's cool, drinkin' our coffee. Sit down, gal. Just made this cake yest'day; cut yourself a piece."

"Thanks, no; I'm not hungry," said Margaret. She looked about at the other women, at Mrs. Holbrooks, stout, dressed in her best Sunday black silk. Mrs. King, tremendously tall and gaunt, like an old spinster. Mrs. MacKensie, of penurious Scotch descent, a tiny, birdlike woman with pecking manners and a reputation for close management of her rich hundred acres. And then the stranger, Lydia Holbrooks, a slender and dainty young girl of about Margaret's age. It was upon her that Margaret fixed her intent regard. The girl wore a soft and flowing dress of rose-sprigged muslin with a demure collar of rose ribbons high about her throat; a tiny flower-trimmed bonnet of lace and ribbons was tilted forward over her low white forehead and chestnut curls and was tied coquettishly under her round white chin. She was very tiny and beautifully made; for the rest, she had a piquant little face like a saucy child's, all dainty white and pink, with large blue eyes charmingly wide.

Margaret saw nothing but this town-bred girl, whose father was one of the wealthiest men of Williamsburg, a book and newspaper publisher. And as she looked down at the girl, who returned her fierce regard with impudent amusement, she felt her gorge rise at her own awkward-ness, her outgrown dress, her strong brown hands. She felt herself to be unutterably ugly, her hair slipping down her sunburned neck. Her face turned scarlet; she could have died in her shame and self-loathing.

"So glad to know you," Lydia murmured. "You're Maggie, aren't you?"

Margaret mechanically took the hand; it was lost in her strong brown fingers. She relinquished it as though it were a snake. Lydia smiled again. What a great gawk! she was thinking. And they were silly enough to think that dear John Hobart would run after this lumbering country wench!

The others, with the exception of Mrs. Holbrooks, Lydia's aunt, smirked knowingly at each other. Mrs. King actually tittered in a smothered voice; Mrs. MacKensie raised sandy eyebrows, like little wings, far up on her tranquil forehead. Each lady smoothed her best Sunday silk dress with conscious hands. But Mrs. Holbrooks looked at Margaret with a sort of angry pity. She had a large and meticulously kept house; she ruled her household of meek husband and three hired men with a hand of iron; she was close and hard; but under her hardness she was just and even kind.

Now her gray eyes snapped. She gave Mrs. King such a glance that that lady subsided, her mouth open with injured amazement. Mrs. Holbrooks had no use for the shiftless Hamiltons; she despised and berated them on all occasions. She had shown no charity in flaying Margaret, either today or in the yesterdays. But now, looking at the girl, her slender and beautiful figure hidden by the childish gingham dress, the white stockings corrugated on her really delicate ankles, the frayed pink sunbonnet revealing unruly masses of black hair, she was conscious of a wrathful compassion. Why, dress that girl up, wash her face, fix her hair decently, and her own husband's niece, (of whom she was very fond) would look a cheap little hussy in comparison! Mrs. Holbrooks' eyes were sharp and saw what others did not see.

"Sit down, Maggie!" she snapped. "Coffee's still hot; anyone can drink coffee."

No one made an effort to give Margaret a cup of coffee, so Mrs. Holbrooks, with sharp gestures, poured out a cup. Margaret took it, sipped at it; her lips were white and trembling.

"Ain't it hot, walkin' over them hills?" asked Mrs. Holbrooks. Her eyes flayed the others, and they started nervously.

"Yes, it's hot," murmured Margaret. She wanted to

strike back at them; instead she sat there, trembling before them.

"How's your Maw?" queried Mrs. MacKensie, agitatedly following Mrs. Holbrooks' lead.

Margaret, getting partial command over herself, turned her blazing eyes on the woman, and Mrs. MacKensie shrank.

"Say, now, this is my niece, Lydia Holbrooks," Mrs. Holbrooks said briskly. "Visitin' me for a couple weeks. Whyn't you come over some day and visit a while with her, Maggie?"

"I'm busy," said Margaret.

"You're not getting married, are you?" Lydia asked in her clear, sweet voice. Her eyes danced with amusement; they slithered away from Margaret and drew the other women into the charmed circle of her laughter at this ugly creature.

"No," answered Margaret calmly. "Are you?" Lydia flushed, looked startled. "Not yet," she replied impudently. "But then, I'm only eighteen. I've lots of time."

"I'm nineteen," remarked Margaret; she could even smile a little now.

Lydia raised her fine black brows. "Are you, now?" she asked with a great assumption of innocent surprise. "I thought you to be at least twenty-six. That's why I asked if you were going to be married."

Then Margaret laughed. She felt herself rapidly rising above the situation.

"We let the men do the courting in this country," she said. Lydia turned scarlet; Mrs. Holbrooks smiled sourly.

"Really, aren't you being a little offensive?" asked Lydia.

"No. Aren't you?" came the tranquil retort.

Lydia was unpleasantly surprised. This horrid girl spoke, not in the accents of rural ignorance, but in a modulated and cultivated voice.

"I'm sure I didn't mean to be offensive," said Lydia stiffly. "I hope I am a lady."

"I hope so, too," remarked Margaret softly. She shrugged a little. "But then, one never knows, does one?"

In the appalled silence that followed, Mrs. Holbrooks laughed raucously. She leaned over and patted Margaret's knee.

"Oh, you're a great one, ain't you, Maggie? Come on, now, you girls, stop your backbitin'. You ought to be friends."

"I'm sure I'm always ready to be friends with ladies of my own class," said Lydia venomously.

Margaret looked at her straightly; in that regard was utter contempt.

"Yes, one should always stick to her own class, shouldn't she?" she replied serenely. Lydia gasped; but Margaret turned to Mrs. Holbrooks and smiled sweetly.

"I hear you bought that prize bull in Whitmore over John Hobart's bidding," she remarked. "John was very much annoyed."

Mrs. Holbrooks grinned; she drew Margaret into a secret fellowship. Her eyes sparkled. "Close-fisted young devil," she chuckled. "I outwitted him that time, though. They'll have to get up early in the mornin' to git ahead of old Martha Holbrooks!"

Lydia had recovered; she returned to the attack.

"I hear you know a friend of mine, John Hobart," she said flutingly. "Such a wonderful man! But, perhaps you don't know him. Would you, now?"

"I would—now," answered Margaret. Lydia lifted her brows with an affectation of extreme surprise, and her glance went slowly and pointedly over Margaret's poor clothing.

"I wouldn't have thought it!" she murmured. "But then, in the country one knows almost everyone. One can't avoid one's neighbors, I suppose. We draw lines, in the city."

"I suppose that is a good thing," said Margaret. She was completely in command of herself now. "In the country we are compelled to meet and endure all kinds of people with courtesy, if nothing else. In the city, I, for instance, would be more particular."

This completely floored Lydia; tears rose passionately into her pretty blue eyes. But Mrs. MacKensie attacked now. She almost winked at the other women and did not look directly at Margaret.

"I bin hearin' Johnny Hobart's goin' to git married," she said. "You wouldn't know anythin' 'bout that, would ye, Maggie?"

"I did hear something," replied Margaret indifferently.

Susan chuckled. She looked at her niece. "Folks used to say you might be the one he was amarryin', though I allus said no to 'em. It's funny, ain't it?"

"Very funny," agreed Margaret tranquilly. If she had not heard the conversation before she entered this house, she would have been exquisitely amused. Now, the sharp anguish twisted again in her breast, and against her will her eye turned to Lydia.

Lydia laughed trillingly and fanned herself with her lace-edged handkerchief.

"Oh, that's too funny!" she cried, abandoning once and for all her well-bred caution. "Too funny for words! I'm sure you are all mistaken! Why, only a little while ago, when I met him at a friend's house, he didn't seem to have any definite intentions, though he *did* ask permission to call on Mamma and Papa!"

Margaret's face had turned extremely white. Mrs. Holbrooks, seriously alarmed, seized the rudder of conversation. "Maggie, I'm sorry to hear about your Granny's death," she said hurriedly. "It was sudden, wasn't it?"

For one moment she was compassionately afraid that Margaret would do something dreadful which would give these harpies, young and old, an opportunity to destroy her. But the girl's eyes, though stricken, were steady.

"Very sudden," she replied quietly. "I'll never stop missing her." She stood up. "I must go, now. It's getting late." She picked up her bonnet.

"Oh, Maggie, you ain't goin' 'thout seein' Ralph, be you?" exclaimed Susan without looking at her niece. She glanced at her visitors; one lashless lid slipped partially over an eye. "He'll be real cross if he missed you."

Margaret made no reply.

"Didn't you say your boy was agoin' away?" asked Mrs. King in her sharp, thin voice.

Susan sniffled dolefully yet proudly. "Yes. He says there ain't no opportunity for what he wants to do roundabouts here," she answered mysteriously. Then her expression became somewhat uneasy. She had pinched the sum of thirty dollars for Ralph from the sale of her farm produce; this was unknown to Silas, of whom she was mortally afraid. But before anyone could speak again, Ralph himself darkened the door of the "settin' room."

For a moment, dazzled by the sun outside, he could not distinguish one woman from another. But he knew that there were strangers there. He turned to go.

"Come in, son," called Susan. Her drawn face became soft and proud.

He murmured something about not meaning to intrude, then he saw Margaret. Instantly his face became illuminated.

"Margaret!" he exclaimed. "I didn't see you!"

He came into the room. He saw no one but his cousin, who smiled at him tenderly.

"Son!" cried Susan, with an angry glance at her niece. "Don't you see we got comp'ny? And this gal here is Miss Lydia Holbrooks, from Williamsburg, Mis' Holbrooks' niece."

The sudden glory still stained Ralph's face as he turned dutifully to Lydia, who gave him her tiny hand coquettishly. He looked at her unseeingly.

"Dear! I didn't know you had such handsome young men in this country!" exclaimed Lydia. "Otherwise I would have come before."

At the prodding of his mother, Ralph sat down uneasily. He still looked at Margaret, who stood in the center of the room.

"Didn't you say you must be goin'?" asked Susan sharply.

"Yes. But I want to talk to Ralph for a minute," replied Margaret calmly. She, too, seated herself. There was a long hard pause. Then Lydia, with a sprightly attempt to draw the youth out, engaged him in vivacious conversation. He replied courteously in a voice that sounded as though it came from behind a wall.

During the conversation that followed, Margaret sat
in silence. Her need to see him, to talk with him, to touch
his hand began to fade, and in its place came a kind of
contempt, as she watched his egotism emerge. His voice
took on a conscious precision that made her want to slap
him. She knew that Ralph was assuming the role of the
poet and the superior, delicate soul; she wondered why
he had never seemed so inadequate to her before.

She stood. "I 'spect Ma isn't coming, after all," she said.
She nodded slightly. "Well, good evening, I'm going."

She marched out of the room, stepped firmly on the
porch. She began to walk toward the hills. Then she
heard running steps behind her and turned. Ralph was
panting in her wake.

"Wait, Margaret!" he called. She waited in silence. He
came up to her, his light hair bobbing over his forehead.
He sighed.

"Thought I could never get away! God, what dull, unimportant people!"

Still in silence, Margaret resumed her walk toward the
hills, her cousin following. They started to climb. Neither
spoke again until they reached the top of the hill. They
sat down under the shade of a clump of second-growth
timber. The sun was beginning to sink; the valley below
was dreaming.

"I'm leaving here October first," began Ralph abruptly.
"We can be married in Whitmore, Margaret."

She opened her mouth to speak, then closed it.

He went on, not even looking at her, "I'm sick to death
of this place and these God-forsaken cattle! I want to get
out, to see things, strange places, adventure. What is there
here for a man who has any kind of a brain at all? Nothing! And then sometimes I think what if I do get out?
What if the world is just the way it is here, just work,
work, nothing but a bore to a man like me?"

"Did it ever occur to you that you're a damn bore most
of the time, yourself?" exclaimed Margaret. "You make
me tired, Ralph! What have you done that gives you the
right to be bored? I've been after you for ages to send your
poems away to some publisher, and you look faintly su-

perior and say, 'They wouldn't understand them.' Perhaps not. It's because I believe you really don't understand anything, yourself." She breathed deeply. "How can anyone with eyes be bored in a world like this! Look at it! Don't you see anything?"

He was coldly enraged now. Margaret had never turned against him before.

"I see as much as you do!" he cried. "More perhaps. That's why most people bore me. Creatures without substance, without mind. Just human breeding and working machines—"

"You neither breed nor work!" said Margaret shortly. "What's wrong with breeding, anyway? Those people who breed, who work with their hands, have made it possible for you to be alive, to eat, to have a bed to sleep in, without you doing very much about it yourself."

He went white with anger.

"Is that what you think? My God, do you think I want it that way? I thought you understood, Margaret. I thought you knew that I want to work as well as any other man, but not just plowing and milking cows. Poetry is my work, Margaret; it's what was meant for me."

"You've got to go away, Ralph," she said. "The sooner, the better. You've got to go where you can find yourself, stand on your own feet, learn to live. You'll never learn to live here."

His face brightened, and he caught her hand. "We'll go to Whitmore, as we always said, and be married when we leave. I can't go before October, though. Maybe it'll be hard at first, but we'll get along. Margaret, you do love me, don't you?"

She put her hand on his neck. He smiled at her and kissed the palm of her hand. At the touch she was suffused with gentleness. Yes, of course she loved him.

John Hobart! What had she to do with him? Standing there, her hand still on Ralph's neck, she felt a swift distaste for John, a repudiation. Had she actually suffered at the words of that stupid Lydia Holbrooks? It was incredible. Let her have John if she wanted him; she, Margaret, wanted nothing of him.

She put her hands on his shoulders, shook him slightly and humorously. "Well, it's October, isn't it? Not long; we must have some patience. Kiss me, Ralph."

Eagerly, he leaned forward to obey her, but she suddenly drew back from him.

In the clear sunset air the white road that wound between the hills was sharply visible. She had recognized, from its glitter and the shine of its red wheels, the carryall of the Holbrooks'. Mrs. Holbrooks and her niece were returning home. And from the opposite direction a horseman was approaching. It was John Hobart, on the way to visit Margaret. She saw the carryall draw to a stop; she saw the horseman stop beside it. At length the carryall started again, and with it, the horseman! He had wheeled his horse about; he was going to the Holbrooks'. Once his rollicking bellow of laughter rose distantly to Margaret's ears. In a few moments they vanished behind the shoulder of a hill.

An icy coldness fell over Margaret. Everything became a little dark.

"Margaret!" said Ralph, who had seen nothing. "What is it?"

She touched him lightly on the shoulder. He was amazed at her expression, rigid and wild. She turned and left him, running down the hill toward her home. He called after her repeatedly; she gave no answer or sign.

Peter had not yet returned when she reached the house. But in the kitchen the children were fighting over their supper of cold biscuits and fried pork. Margaret entered; Melinda began to question her. Margaret made one fierce gesture, then went into the "settin' room."

She sat down on the bed. She was shivering as though the room were cold. She pushed back her hair vaguely.

Then at last she sat perfectly immobile, staring with dead eyes before her.

Chapter Six

JOHN HOBART DID NOT come on Monday. Neither did he come on Tuesday. On Wednesday, Mrs. Holbrooks gave a party for her niece and invited nearly everyone in the county. Everyone but the Hamiltons.

On Wednesday evening, at sunset, Peter came home from his smithy, his face black and menacing. His blood-shot eyes fell on Margaret as she stood cooking the evening meal at the dirty stove. The children swarmed about her, and he swept them from his path.

"What's this I hear about John Hobart runnin' after that Holbrooks hussy?" he roared. "Ezra King came 'round today for the fust time in a spell, with two hosses. I knowed right away he wanted to say somethin' to me, cuz he takes his hosses over to Bartlet. And there he stood grinnin' at me like a dirty possum, and he sez, ' 'Spect Johnny Hobart's got sick o' runnin' after your gal Maggie. He's makin' eyes at Miss Lydia Holbrooks now, and folks do say it's a match. Know anythin' about it, Pete?' I don't say nothin', rememberin' you and John don't want nothin' said just yet, though God knows why! But what I want to know is this: what you done to Johnny Hobart? He ain't been here since the old woman died. What you done, eh?"

Margaret turned the pork over carefully in the skillet and absently waved away the clustering flies. It was too dim in the kitchen for Peter to see her expression.

"Nothin's wrong," she said carelessly. "He'll be 'round. Not tonight, though, on account of that party Mis' Holbrooks' givin'. 'Course he's got to go; he knows Lydia Holbrooks, from Williamsburg."

Peter seized her arm; swung her roughly around to face him. With fury, he peered into her face.

"You lie!" he bellowed. "Don't you try any of your tricks on me, wench, or I'll break every bone in your body! I'll—"

His menacing voice broke off abruptly. He stared at Margaret; she could no longer hide her anguish and the set despair of her lips. There was something in her eyes so tragic that Peter's own eyes narrowed. The clutch on her arm slackened, became a gentle hold. But his face took on grimness.

"Maggie," he said huskily, "if that skunk's jilted you, made the whole country laugh at you, hurt you, I'll—I'll have his guts out!"

"I tell you, it's goin' to be all right," answered Margaret dully, shrugging off her father's arm. "Leave me be. You'll see: he'll be here tomorrow sometime."

And John Hobart did come "tomorrow," at sunset.

He came, unseen by the other members of the family. Peter had not yet returned. The children were fighting on the stoop. He passed the barn, and through the wide doorway he saw Margaret milking the cows. Her head was bent, the falling braids obscuring her face; she worked stolidly, her shoulders slack. Once she drew a deep, convulsive breath.

John whistled, stepped heavily into the gloom of the barn. She started visibly, glanced up. He was surprised at the pallor of her face, and then at the crimson flood that flowed over it. He grinned.

"Howdy, Maggie!" he almost shouted. He stooped over her, kissed her lips resoundingly. She could feel the bristles about his mouth; her lips were cold under his. He stood, peering at her in the gloom with narrowed eyes.

"What's wrong?" he demanded.

She smiled; her face felt stiff and numb. She could not speak; she thought that if she tried just now she would burst into uncontrolled weeping. So she merely clutched his sleeve in wet and slipping fingers. How good to feel the rough strong fabric between her fingers! She stood up, pushing her hair back from her face. She could speak, now.

"Nothin's wrong, John," she said quietly. "You just frightened me a little. I didn't hear you come."

He stared at her, enchanted and gratified. He took her in his arms, kissed her again and again. Her knees turned to water as they always did at his touch; her lips warmed under his; her arms slowly slipped around his neck.

And thus Peter, tramping heavily past the barn, saw them. His surly face lighted a little; after a moment he entered the barn, placated but still surly.

John grinned at him as he relinquished Margaret. "Hi there, ole timer!" he cried.

"Ole, yourself," muttered Peter. He glanced swiftly at Margaret; he shrewdly appraised the change in her face. He turned to John, frowning.

"Where you been? Heerd you was chasin' after the Holbrooks' wench. Call that a right way to treat my daughter, eh?"

John stared; he burst into a roar of laughter.

"So that was what was the matter with Maggie, here!" he said, pleased. "Well, I'll be damned!"

"You would have been if you hadn't shown yourself here tonight!" said Peter grimly. "Well, what you got to say, eh?"

John still laughed, and looked at Margaret, but she was eying her father as though she wished to annihilate him.

"Well, that's a good un!" John went on. "Jealous o' that bit of cheap town silk! I'll be damned!" he exclaimed, more and more delighted. "I ain't sayin' the gal didn't try to ketch me. She did. But she ain't the first gal's set her cap for John Hobart, and prob'ly won't be the last, neither, until me and Mag gets hitched!"

"Yes, that's just it," broke in Peter, glowering again. "What's behind all this 'bout not tellin' anybody, and makin' Mag the joke o' the whole countryside? Eh?"

John looked stolidly at Margaret as he replied, "Tain' my idea. Maggie, here, can tell you that, herself. I wanted to marry her a week ago, but, no, she wouldn't have it 'till that cousin of hers left the county. Ain't that right, Mag?"

Peter turned enragedly to his daughter. She nodded

calmly. "That's right, Pa. I won't have Ralph hurt. He wanted to marry me; he's goin' away and I'm goin' to have him go 'thout tellin' him anythin'. He'll learn soon enough."

"Oh, so you won't have him hurt, won't you!" growled Peter dangerously. "Of all the damn foolishness! Wal, let me tell you, I'm goin' to town tonight and tell ev'rybody I see that you agoin' to marry John Hobart, and damn soon, too!"

"No, you won't, 'less Maggie says you kin," said John quietly.

Chapter Seven

Margaret did not repeat the incident of the little hollow despite urgings from John, and his baffled anger.

"You know there ain't no one but you for me, Maggie," he would urge. "You know how damned bad I want you, need you!"

"You'll want me and need me more when we're married, then," she would answer.

Much excited conjecture went on in the county. John's new house was already being built, not far from the old one, which was to be demolished. The best rough white stone was already standing in heaps about the site; five "town" builders and laborers worked with significant haste. Farmers gathered in the copper glow of the autumn evenings about the place, smoking and chatting, and guardedly rallying John, who was a hard-eyed taskmaster and watched every stone go into place.

The consensus was that the Holbrooks gal had "hooked" him. At any rate, she extended her visit well past the first week in October, and John was seen to be very attentive at every house where they met. He even went very frequently to visit old Holbrooks, ostensibly, but rumors were about that the visit usually ended up with John and Lydia whispering and laughing together in a dim corner, not too rigidly chaperoned by the grimly pleased Mis' Holbrooks. When other women and girls teased Lydia about this, she would blush but say nothing. In reality, she was not satisfied; John flirted with her, led her on, but said nothing definite. In her own room, she would burst into irritable tears. Nevertheless, she was certain she would get him.

It was conceded by everyone, finally, that the wedding would take place very soon. Lydia began thinking of the trip she and her Mamma would take to New York for the trousseau. She drove out one day to look at the partially completed new house, and criticized prettily. John merely grinned. She went home with her aunt, pleased and elated, fluttering her dainty handkerchief at John as the carriage bore her off.

Peter heard all this, and roared angrily at Margaret when he returned home. She made no reply. His only consolation was the visits of John at night.

As for Margaret, her mental distress had reached a point of hot irritation and despair. For Ralph did not leave his home the first of October. It was well into the middle of the month, and he still did not leave. It was a matter of money. He had decided that with a wife he would need more than thirty dollars. He had not told his mother of his plans with regard to Margaret; he merely urged her to try to squeeze extra money away from Silas Rowe, whom he hated passionately.

Things, therefore, were in a universally dissatisfied state. John, balked, became increasingly resentful, Peter more unmanageable, Margaret more desperate. She was torn with furies.

One fury was the returned love for her cousin when she was not with John. A thousand times her decision wavered. Tossed to and fro by her storms of physical desire when with John, and overcome with tenderness when with Ralph, her life was miserable.

Toward the end of October, Margaret suddenly awakened one morning with the knowledge that she was pregnant.

The realization appalled her. She dressed with wet hands, ran to the barn where she could be alone, away from the swarming of her family. She paced back and forth, pushing her hair vaguely from her face, sobbing under her breath. There could be no more delay now; she had to marry John.

Instantly, she was conscious of a surge of relief that the decision was finally out of her hands. With a calm face she returned to the house.

She and Ralph still met on odd nights when John did not come. This particular night, she told herself, she must settle things.

She met Ralph just as the shortening autumn twilight was settling on the hills. Watching him climb slowly up the other side of the hill, her heart failed her, and she ran down to him with her hands outstretched in despairing love.

He was surprised at the haggardness of her face. He let her assist him up the hill, then sat down beside her. She looked at him fixedly.

"Ralph, I can't wait any longer. Aren't you ready to go, yet?"

He flushed, dropped his eyes. "Not yet. But I'll be ready in a couple of weeks, I think."

She almost sobbed in her despair.

"Ralph, you've got to be ready, right away. Do you hear, right away? If you love me, as you say you do, you've got to be ready, now!"

"I'm sorry, I can't just yet," he said tightly.

A silence fell. The hills were ruddy with the last dying light. Margaret stared at them dully, her head fallen almost on her breast. Finally she looked at Ralph again, and her eyes filled with tears.

"Ralph," she said gently, "what's the trouble?"

"If you want to know," he burst out, "I haven't got enough money. Money! Everything is damned money!"

"Ralph," she said softly. "Listen. I—I've got about twenty dollars of my own." He turned to her in amazement, joy creeping into his face. "I—I'll meet you here tomorrow night, and give it to you . . ."

"Margaret!" He seized her hand, kissed it. "Margaret! Then, we can go tomorrow night! Oh, thank God for that! Margaret, you don't know what I've suffered!"

And you don't know what I've suffered, she thought grimly. "See, Ralph," she said aloud, "there's a train for Williamsburg at ten o'clock tomorrow night. Bring all your things with you; be ready to start out. And I'll meet you here, at about sundown. That'll give you—us—about three hours to get to Whitmore and catch the train."

His joy made him incoherent. He kissed her shyly and repeatedly like a delighted small boy. She let him hold her, and she returned his gentle caresses. When she left him, she felt that she had grown very old.

The next afternoon John came, and found Margaret digging the last of the potatoes out of the patch. She knelt in the earth, grimy and hot, and absorbed, apparently, in her work. When she saw him coming over the fields, she stood up and awaited him in silence.

He was hard to manage these days. Though she smiled at him, he merely looked at her stonily, then shifted his gaze to the ground. She took him playfully by the arm.

"John," she said softly. "Would you like to tell everybody tomorrow that you and I are going to be married next week?"

He stared at her unbelievingly. Then he caught her by the shoulders.

"D'ye mean it, Mag? By God, d'ye mean it?"

"Yes, I mean it. Tomorrow."

He put his arms about her; she could feel that he was trembling through all his big body. She allowed him to kiss her bruisingly. Then she pushed him away a little.

"John," she said soberly, "I—I've got to ask you a favor. Somethin' you can do for me. Will you?"

John released her slowly. "What is it?"

"John. Listen to me. Ralph is goin' to go away tonight; he won't come back. But he hasn't enough money—"

"So, the yeller dog sent you to ask me to give him money!" snapped John. "Wal, I'm damned if I—"

"No, that isn't so! John, he doesn't know I'm not goin' with him; he doesn't know I'm askin' this of you. He'll never know. But, if he doesn't get the money, he won't go; I told him I had it, myself. He wants to wait until he gets it. I can't let him stay here and see me marry you. He'll learn soon enough about us. Perhaps it won't hurt so, then, when he's in a strange place and has to stand on his own two feet, himself. He'll learn to depend on himself—"

"He'll never learn that!" exclaimed John harshly,

but Margaret's words had moved him. He gnawed his lip a moment. "You think he'll get backbone when he gets away, but he won't! He'll never have that. He'll get someone else to lean on." He paused. "How much d'ye want?"

Margaret sighed with relief. "About twenty dollars," she said.

"That's a heap of money," he said. He pulled out his sturdy old leather purse, counted out twenty dollars, handed them to Margaret. She took them; the money seemed to burn her fingers. When she glanced up at him, he was regarding her fixedly, his eyes speculative. She had an impulse to hurl the money into his face, to turn from him and run, and never see him again. Instead, she looked at him calmly.

"Thank you," she said quietly. She put the money in her apron pocket. Then she began to dig the potatoes again.

Ralph was waiting for Margaret. The autumn twilight was setting over the valleys and the hollows, filling them with ghostly purple shadows. He waited restlessly. His carpetbag was lying under a young tree; sometimes he glanced at it uneasily.

He heard a faint sound below; he strained his eyes. Yes, there was Margaret climbing the hill below. She was only a shadow, but the sense of her nearness flowed over him, strengthened him. Laughing a little, he met her halfway down, and seized her hands.

"Hurry!" he whispered. "Hurry, hurry!"

It was not until they reached the top again that he saw that she was bareheaded and barefooted, as usual, and that she carried no luggage. He stared at her in the gloom; something cold took a grip on his heart.

"Why, you aren't ready!" he said, his eyes on hers.

She held his hand tightly; its warmth and strength upheld him.

"Let's sit down a minute, dear," she said gently.

"But, you haven't your bag!" The laughter had gone from his voice, he spoke tonelessly.

"Listen, Ralph, dear," she said, stroking his fingers.

"And don't talk until I've finished. My Ma is sick, right sick. I can't leave her right now."

"You're not coming with me?" he said, as if he did not hear the sound of his own voice.

"No, dear, I'm not," she went on gently. "I can't leave her. You see—"

"Then," he cried violently, "I'm not going, either!"

She caught his hand again; held it tightly in both of hers.

"Yes, you're going, Ralph. You've got to go. For more reasons than you know. You—you've got to be a man sometime. I've got to have a man to go to. You—you've got to make a place for me, Ralph. It won't be long. You can do it better if you are free at first. You'll go to Williamsburg and get yourself a job somewhere, and then you'll send for me. It won't be long. You'll be strong, able to handle things for yourself."

He turned his head from her and stared out over the valley.

"Ralph," she said earnestly, "I believe in you. I've always believed in you. You've got to show me that I'm right. You've got to make a place for us. You've got to write me and tell me. I want to be proud of you." Her throat closed up; she could hardly endure her anguish. I'm a dog, she thought. I'm a low, crawling dog.

Ralph wrenched his eyes from the black hills and looked at Margaret for a long time. It was as if he were memorizing her features.

"No, I can't go without you," he said quietly.

She pressed John's money into Ralph's palm; in the dim light he stared at it.

"I'm giving you—my money, dear," she whispered. "You've got to help me out of here."

"I can't go, I tell you. I won't go without you!" his voice began to rise. "You promised me! You lied to me! You never meant to go!"

"Ralph, don't!" She caught him by the arms, forced him down again. He leaned his head against her, and she kissed him tenderly.

"Yes, I meant to go, Ralph. I really meant it. But,

you must see yourself that I can't go just yet. Be strong;
be a man! You can do it. You'll always remember what
I've said to you, Ralph. Always remember it. It's important for you. No matter what happens, say to yourself 'I
am a man.' Nothing can harm you, if you remember
that. And when you go away, you'll take me along with
you, even if you don't see me. You'll always remember
that I love you, and then, someday, you'll understand;
you'll say, that's all she could have done; she could have
done nothing else."

An ear less tuned inward to his own thoughts would
have heard in her words a farewell. But his self-conceit
drank up her words even in his despair.

However, he was still not reconciled. He kissed her,
again and again and because of the strength she had in-
fused in him, he became evanescently strong. She was
very tired. Slowly she sank back on the damp soft leaves;
his head blotted out the sky above her eyes; he kissed her
lips repeatedly.

She did not know that she was crying until she heard
his comforting words, uttered in a voice newly mascu-
line.

Her supine lassitude, the attitude of surrender she
made, aroused passion for the first time in Ralph, a weaker shadow of John's passion, but a strong passion just
the same. Awakened now to amazement, Margaret felt his
breath in her face, felt the beating of his heart against her
own. New, too, was the power in his possessing arms, the
iron strength of them.

She thought, He wants me, poor Ralph. He wants me
for the first time in his life. But, how can I? I don't feel
anything, not a thing. But if I do, I shall send Ralph
away, strong and satisfied, so that when he hears about
me and John, he'll still be strong.

And yet, as she thought this, she was conscious of a
sudden physical revulsion. It amazed her dully; she loved
him, but she wished he would stop kissing her. She felt
a guilt as though she were about to do something inde-
cent, something that violated her, and her amazement
rose again that contact with John had never shamed her.

Then, because of her compassion, she gave herself to Ralph, with a queer sorrow that she could not return his ardor, could only lie in his arms, cold and unresponsive. Shame overwhelmed her, and because of this she simulated surrender and love, so that he might not guess.

The moonless sky was quite dark, sharp with brilliant stars, when Margaret finally murmured that he must go, that it was late. He helped her to her feet; she could feel the assured grip of his hand.

He put his arms around her, held her close.

"You're mine, Margaret, all mine, now. You could never belong to anyone else. I'll come back for you, Maggie, dear. I'll come back soon."

"Yes, you'll come back," she said gently. She kissed him slowly.

He gave her a last kiss, strong and forceful; she could feel joy in him, an anticipation of conquest. She watched him go. In the starlight, she could see him for quite a distance when he reached the valley. She waved to him; he waved back.

She continued to wave long after she knew he could no longer see her.

Chapter Eight

ALL OF WAYNE COUNTY, and even Jefferson County was electrified. John Hobart, the richest man in three counties, was going to marry that Maggie Hamilton, Peter Hamilton's wild zany of a Maggie!

John had "jilted" Lydia Holbrooks; no, Lydia had jilted John. No! There'd never been anythin' between the two, it was only Maggie; John said so himself.

Lydia had great fortitude for so little a creature. When her uncle, Seth Holbrooks, came in and whispered the news to his wife, and she had then gently broken it to Lydia, the girl had merely become stiff and white for a moment, and then she had smiled.

"I don't believe it!" she had said lightly, but her stricken eyes told that she believed it. She immediately began to pack her bags; she would have none of her aunt's comforting; her manner repelled sympathy.

"Seth says they're asayin' over the county that you jilted John," urged Mrs. Holbrooks, "and that he's marryin' Maggie Hamilton now, out of spite. You've got to stay, Lydia, so that they'll believe it."

"But it isn't true!" cried the girl bitterly, not looking at her aunt. "It isn't true! And no one'll believe it, even if I do stay." She began to cry, chokingly.

"If you run away, lovie, they'll know it ain't true. But if you stay and smile like you can and pretend to be gay, they'll never know."

And so she stayed.

Most agitated of all was Susan Blodgett. She had hardly heard the news from Si Rowe, when she had made him hitch up the horse and drive her over to her sister's. She found Melinda triumphant and smug. Susan burst in on her like a thin torrent of icy rain, weakly raving and furious. Peter happened to be home at the time, eating his midday meal, and he listened with a broad grin. But after a few moments, his face became grim.

"T'was only yesterday, Melindy, mind you, only yesterday, and Ralph tells me, 'Ma, I'm agoin' away, and Maggie's comin' with me. We're goin' away together.' I didn't believe it; if I'd believed it, I would've come right over, and tried to stop it. But Si says, 'Let him shoot his mouth off; he's only a boy. That gal wouldn't go with him.' I knowed Ralph was goin', but I didn't know just when, and then this mornin' I found him gone, and a note sayin' he was agoin' with your Maggie. I nigh had a stroke, and Si had to throw water in my face, and right when I was ascreamin' for him to hitch up and take me over here, in walks Ezra King, grinnin' from ear to ear, and he says, 'Hear the news? Johnny Hobart's weddin' Pete's Maggie!'

"And now, Melindy, as you're my born sister, d'ye think that's right of your Maggie to be tellin' my poor Ralph that she's agoin' with him, gettin' him to leave his pore old mother, and then not goin' with him?"

"Here!" shouted Peter, rising like a great bear and glowering down at the woman. "First you yammer that my gal's run off with your damn precious pup, and then you yammer because she didn't run off with him! And see here, you old witch, I won't have you talkin' about my Maggie as if she's dirt; she's a Hamilton, hear? A Hamilton wouldn't dirty her feet with the likes of your baby boy. And now you'll shut your yap, or I'll shut it for you!" He stamped out of the house, muttering fiercely.

Susan began to weep. Sitting side by side in the little kitchen, the sisters looked exactly alike, both scrawny, shrunken, and livid, except that Susan was better and more neatly dressed.

"It ain't right," Susan moaned over and over, wiping her eyes.

"It ain't right," Melinda moaned, wiping her nose.

They belabored the absent Maggie with vicious words, and when little blue-eyed Linda strolled in, Melinda caught her feverishly to her shrunken breast, began to stroke her face with hot and trembling hands. Over and over, to the bewildered child, she said that her sister was a bad girl, and Linda looked at them solemnly. She could not reconcile the marriage of Margaret to rich Johnny Hobart as being bad, but if her Ma said so, it must be so.

The ladies went over in a body to the Holbrooks' farm, ostensibly to console Lydia delicately, but in reality to see how "she was takin' it, she bein' so dead set on him." They found Lydia quite calm, though a little pinkish about the eyes. She talked to them carelessly, her tongue amusedly barbed and disinterested when she spoke of Maggie. But she did not deceive the sharp-eyed country dames. They went away, tittering among themselves, not at all displeased to have been witness to a little scene of grief.

But no one dared voice his opinion to John Hobart. People contented themselves in rallying him cautiously and respectfully about his coming marriage. If he knew their opinions, he despised them too completely to care. A man who holds the mortgage on almost every farm in the county has too great a sense of power to consider the opinions of those he holds in financial bondage. Moreover, he was too happy.

Then, with a large gesture, he invited the whole county to his wedding.

Three days before the wedding, Mesdames Holbrooks, Brownlow, MacKensie, and King called upon the bride. With them came Lydia, in flowered muslin over pink silk, her rose velvet hat nodding with pink roses. She held a ruffled pink parasol over her head.

This was the first time in years that anyone had paid a formal call upon Melinda Hamilton, and when the smart buggies wound about the dusty white road and made for the shack, she was overcome with mingled dismay and gratification. Margaret was washing a huge tubful of dirty clothes behind the house, and Melinda shrilled at her:

"Maggie! Come in and put your Sunday clo'es on! Mis' Holbrooks and Mis' King and Mis' MacKensie and Mis' Brownlow's comin! Dear, dear, you look a sight!"

Margaret's best dress consisted of a simple white muslin which she had made two years before, almost transparent now from repeated scrubbings. She tied the wide sash with an angry jerk, not realizing how the pale fabric highlighted her dark loveliness. She put on her white cotton stockings and black slippers. By this time she had reached a stage of fatalistic despair. She combed her hair rapidly, the black waves of it rippling almost to her knees. She pushed it severely behind her ears, then caught it up in a huge and shining mass at the nape of her neck. Only then did she wash her face, and it emerged from the caustic suds a clear brown, stained with scarlet on the cheekbones. Then she went in to the guests.

For a moment they stood dazzled by unusual beauty and dignity. They had all dressed in their Sunday best, but before this young woman in her plain, white gown, they became commonplace.

Mrs. Holbrooks was the first to speak.

"Howdy, Maggie, my dear. Thought we'd come and give you our good wishes for when you marry Johnny Hobart."

"Thank you," answered Margaret quietly. She smiled at all the ladies present. Lydia gave her her hand sweetly, letting a slight smile of derision struggle on her face.

Mrs. Holbrooks regarded Margaret with kindliness.

"Johnny Hobart's a fine man, Maggie. I hope you'll be very happy. And, somehow, I think he's gettin' the best of the bargain, after all."

Margaret smiled, plaited her fingers together. She glanced at her mother, in her perpetual gray shawl, and hated her, hated her snifflings, her nervous affectations of manners. She was chattering in a high shrill voice, about "bein' so surprised, Maggie goin' away and all, but when gals sets their minds on gettin' married, 'spect they didn't ask their Ma's permission."

Oh, shut up! thought Margaret with her father's savagery.

"Yes, it was a surprise," said Lydia sweetly. She played prettily with the ivory handle of her closed parasol, and, catching Margaret's eye, looked with insolent significance about the wretched room. The late autumn sunlight glowed redly on the dusty windows; flies swarmed in the illuminated dust motes. Lydia shrank in her splintered chair, lifted the hem of her dress fastidiously.

Margaret wanted to order them out of the house. They had come to see, to go off together shaking with mirth, to shake their heads. Stupid fools, with their hands folded stiffly in their laps, as though afraid of contagion!

When they had gone, she felt suddenly broken. There had been nothing in the house to offer the guests. The children, drawn home by an acute sense of something happening, had scuffled on the stoop, and had peered into the room at the visitors. Everything had had a nightmarish quality.

All she desired was relief from the dull ache in her breast.

Chapter Nine

THERE HAD NEVER BEEN such a grand wedding in the
the memory of the county.

John had "done himself proud." The new barn, huge,
and smelling of sap and sawdust, was lighted with a score
of lamps and lanterns. The floor had been waxed for
dancing. John had engaged a real group of waltz-musi-
cians from Whitmore; five fiddlers, a harpist, and a
drummer. A temporary platform had been built to hold
the musicians and the platform itself was covered ele-
gantly with turkey-red carpet. A table had been prepared
to hold punch and glass cups in one corner of the barn.
Streamers of red, white, and blue ribbon decorated every
post, and even trailed downward from the roof.

John's housekeeper was his paternal aunt, Miss Betsy
Hobart, an old woman with a forbidding face, steel eye
glasses, and a rigid, humorless mouth. She kept his house
meticulously and was an excellent cook. She had said no
word to John about Margaret when he had been pur-
suing her, though her opinion of the Hamiltons was very
low. He never knew her opinion of the marriage.

Miss Betsy had a hired girl; to help with the cooking
and the festivities, she engaged three more girls tem-
porarily. For four days they had all been working. Fresh
curtains stood at the windows of the old gray-timbered
house. The antique walnut and mahogany had been
polished until it glittered; in the dining room the table
had been laid with a cloth as stiff as satin paper. There
were to be twenty-five guests at the wedding dinner at
five o'clock. Later, after the dancing, there would be extra swarms. Dozens of chickens were slaughtered, the best
hams taken from the cellars, and wine imported from
Williamsburg.

Miss Betsy had been born in this house, and her father before her. She had said nothing about John's plan of demolishing it, but something must have emanated from her, for at the last moment, when the wrecking commenced, he had changed his mind. He told his aunt that she would continue to live in the house. She had merely nodded. But when he had gone, she had wiped a single tear from her eye. The new house stood only half an acre away, green lawns stretching between the two residences. It was only two-thirds finished, without shade, for new saplings had just been planted about it. But the dark old house was sunk deep in the shadow of ancient trees.

Miss Betsy had never been very sociable. Few dared visit the Hobart house except on unusual occasions; the mistress did not encourage social intercourse. There was an old story that she had once been "promised" in her youth to an elegant young man from Williamsburg, but that her father had hated the dandy. He had been a stranger, and how Miss Betsy had met him no one knew. But they did know that he came no more to the Hobart house, and that Miss Betsy, who had been a fine, strapping girl, had never looked at another man. She had kept house for her father and her brother; she had continued to keep house when the older John had brought home some pink-and-white timid little thing from Kentucky, and that she had raised John after his mother had given up the struggle and had died when he was four years old. Whether she loved him or not, John never knew. He really never knew anything about her.

Miss Betsy and Margaret Hamilton had met only half a dozen times in all their lives, but had never spoken. There was something about the older woman which had vaguely frightened Margaret. She had once discussed her with old Margot, but for once the latter was silent, except for one sentence. "There's murder in Betsy."

Margaret had forgotten the strange remark, but on her wedding day she remembered it with an uneasy start. She was to live in the old house, confined therein with Miss Betsy until the new house was finished, which would not be until about Christmas. John had taken her there during a brief absence of Miss Betsy's, and she had remembered the bitter silence, the hush of the carpeted corridors, the green gloom of the shrouding trees at the windows. She had hated it at once, had felt herself an intruder. She became more and more frightened; what would she and Miss Betsy have to say to each other during all the days until the new house was finished? She had no doubt that Miss Betsy hated her, and Miss Betsy's shadow was over all her wedding day. It was only two hours before she was to leave for John's house when Peter, catching a spare moment alone with his daughter, drew her aside.

"Look here, Maggie, there's this thing about old Miss Betsy. She ain't been to visit you like the other folks hereabouts, and ain't never invited you to visit her, neither. Now, they say all kinds of dern things about her, but you got sense, Mag. You don't have to believe nothin'; all you got to do is mind your own business, same as she minds her'n, and you'll git along fine with her. Besides, it ain't long."

"I 'spect she hates me, Pa."

"That's plumb foolishness, Mag. She don't hate you, for the reason that she don't know nothin' about you. If she does hate you, it's becuz she hates most everythin'. Just keep your head and don't make no fusses and everythin' will be all right."

Her father's good common sense heartened Margaret, and she forgot about the forbidding old woman. The Hamilton house was in confusion all that day. The children crowded under everyone's feet and added to the general hysteria. Peter had been able to dig up only twenty-five dollars, and so it was Melinda who had a new purple silk dress, and Linda a cheap white muslin. Margaret had made over old Margot's ivory silk for herself. She trusted the folds of it to conceal her clumsy black slippers.

These last few days Margaret had not thought at all. She was conscious only of haste, of feverish excitement alternating with dull lassitude.

The day was a fair and clear one. An hour before the wedding was to take place, the little church in the hollow began to sound its bell, and the thin clamor of it rolled back from the hills. Margaret heard it as she finished dressing. Her head ached.

John's carryall arrived for the bride's party, which consisted only of the bride, her parents, and her excited younger sister, Linda. Peter wore his greenish-black store clothes. His mighty wrists protruded from the sleeves of his tight coat; his black beard had been decently trimmed, and his broad-brimmed hat had been brushed until the nap was smooth. Melinda felt very elegant in her purple silk and jet bonnet with black streamers; Linda's yellow curls streamed over the white muslin dress. Margaret had found a delicate ivory scarf in her grandmother's box and she held it carefully folded in her hand. Her thoughts were frantic.

God. I'm going to my wedding and it all seems like a nightmare. I wish that bell would stop ringing. I wish I'd let John buy me a real wedding dress. They'll all laugh when I go into the church; Lydia will be there. She'll laugh. I don't blame them. I look a fright. I'm going to be sick, I can feel it. Ralph. Ralph. I'm going to be sick!

Melinda suddenly became conscious that Margaret had not spoken since they had left the house. She glanced at her daughter. The girl's head was averted; she sat straight and stiff, her head bare.

"Time you put on your scarf, Maggie," she said.

After a moment, Margaret's hands listlessly shook out the scarf.

They could see, now, the dozens of buggies and carryalls hitched about the church. No one was visible, for all were inside. From the open door there issued the strains of a wedding march.

From his place before the altar, John could see the blurred faces of his neighbors; he could hear the dull buzz of their whispering, could guess their muttered conjectures. He could think only that in a few minutes Margaret would be his for a lifetime.

The pale gray rectangle of the church door darkened. Margaret and her father were coming in; her hand rested on his arm. Melinda and Linda swooped into seats near the doorway. Margaret and her father were coming down the aisle. Everything became hushed, breathless, except for the wedding march.

Then, from scores of throats came a deep "Ah!" John widened his eyes as he looked at his approaching bride, and was astounded.

She walked proudly, slowly, on her father's arm. Her face was very pale in the gloom of the church. Her tight bodice with its foam of lace at the breast clung smoothly, glistening to every swell of her figure. From the bodice flowed the folds of the ivory silk, gleaming like moonlight in the dusk. On her head was the ivory gossamer of the scarf, and through its meshes could be seen the smooth blackness of her hair. About her throat was clasped the garnet necklace, and from her ears burned the garnet earrings. They threw sharp little scarlet shadows on her flesh, and trembled a little. She was incredibly beautiful.

She moved in a dream. She did not feel the floor under her feet; she floated. She could see John's face, could feel the swift touch of his hand. Otherwise she had lost hold on reality. She heard her voice replying to something in a hush like that of an eternal silence. The organist had tried to pedal down to a faint murmur, and the result was that the instrument had died altogether. There was only the sound of Margaret's voice and John's voice, and, from the distance, a long roll of unseasonable thunder.

The moment the service ended, the rain began, accompanied by a lusty wind. The tin roof of the church rattled like gunfire; lightning glared whitely at the windows. John was kissing Margaret; he was holding her by the arms; he kissed her again and again.

And then it happened. Miss Betsy Hobart rose from her seat in the first pew, an apparition in her black silk dress and bonnet. She came up to the bride and groom; she took Margaret by the arm and turned her about. For a long moment she stared into the girl's face, almost fiercely. Then she leaned forward and kissed Margaret's cheek with her cold, hard lips.

The wedding party rattled merrily away to the Hobart house. The air had turned sharply cool; the earth was silent, the hills dull purple and sodden. But the laughter and voices and calls of the guests echoed clearly, while the sky burned brighter.

The great warm fires in the old house were welcome. Candles and lamps flickered everywhere. Miss Betsy led Margaret up the dimness of the circular staircase to the floor above. Between two tall windows stood the huge white-bed with its four posts; the spread had been folded back, the snowy sheet crisply turned, the pillows immaculate and plump. There was an air of comfort and security in the room.

Margaret put her hand to her head in her old vague gesture and stared about her. The firelight made the old ivory stuff of her gown glow, brought out a hidden grandeur in her figure and face. Miss Betsy watched her from the shadows; then she came forward.

"Look here," she said curtly, and went to the wardrobe. She flung open the door. On various hooks hung several bright feminine dresses of silk and muslin, two new cloaks, and two new bonnets. "These are yours."

"Did John buy those for me before—?"

Miss Betsy closed the door sharply and looked at Margaret with a contemptuous smile.

"No. I did," she replied. Her voice had a hoarse hardness to it.

There was a little silence.

"Thank you," said Margaret uncertainly. Miss Betsy regarded her with fierce gravity.

"I thought, today, that you weren't a fool," she said. "I hope you won't disappoint me. A scoundrel is always better than a fool."

Margaret smiled faintly. "I don't think I'm a scoundrel, but I'm sure I'm not a fool."

"I'm not so sure of it," Miss Betsy said shortly. "See here, that gown of yours won't be any good for dancing.

You'd better put on one of those dresses. I hope they fit you; I think they will. I remembered you well."

Margaret regarded her soberly for some moments.

"Do you know, you remind me of my grandmother," she said suddenly, and then flushed at her words.

"I knew her a little," Miss Betsy said. She retreated to the door, unmoved and a trifle sinister.

Left alone, Margaret removed her wedding gown and put on one of her new dresses, a dark red silk over red merino, which fitted to perfection. She glanced in the mirror, was dreamily amazed at the beauty that gazed back at her, and went down the staircase.

Exclamations of admiration broke from the ladies; the gentlemen merely stared as Margaret entered. John, who was already carving the great hams, glanced up. He stood there, knife in hand, without moving. But Margaret looked at none of the guests, only at Miss Betsy; on the older woman's face there glinted a cold smile of triumph.

In her hushed dreaminess, Margaret was not aware of what she ate, of what she said or did, or whether she smiled or laughed. Neither could she think; at times her eyes closed, and she felt that she was sinking into a deep and cushioned sleep. She would start to consciousness, sounds and voices unbearably sharp in her ears. She was not unaware of the envy and the malice of the women present, but she did not care. She kept telling herself that tomorrow there would be light and sun, and she would be able to fix things securely in her mind.

When the rain had stopped a little there was a rush over the dark moist earth to the barn. It was brightly lighted; the musicians were already playing seductive waltzes and square dances when Margaret entered with John. The gaiety, the laughter, the music, only increased her sense of bemusement.

It was not for some time that she realized Miss Betsy had gone.

On a sudden impulse Margaret opened the door and slipped out into the windy darkness of the night. She ran lightly to the house and as she approached she became aware of the thunderous sound of an organ. She let herself inside and crept softly to the door of the parlor. It stood open; bleak and silent, except for the fire behind the grate and Miss Betsy, rigid and gray at the ancient organ.

Her back was to Margaret, and so she did not see her enter. Her body was stiff and emaciated in the black silk. As though Margaret's entrance were a signal, the organ seemed to draw a tremendous breath, and from it rolled bitter echoes, majestic, heroic, and yet contemptuous. They surged against the walls, rolled back, like a giant that strained at chains. The sound caught at Margaret; involuntarily she put her hands to her ears, shivering, as though the cry came from her and she would suppress it. She was not aware that she was weeping. In that music, she had lost orientation. It was only after a long time that she became aware that everything was silent. She shook her head slightly; as through the mists of a dream she saw that Miss Betsy had turned to her on the organ bench, and that she was looking at her with perfectly expressionless eyes, her hands still on the keys.

Margaret walked to the organ and looked down at the older woman without speaking. They stared into each other's eyes for a long time. It was Miss Betsy who looked away. She smiled a little grimly.

"Child, what are you doing, coming back here?" she asked.

"I don't know," the girl answered quietly. She rubbed the old mahogany of the instrument with the palm of her hand.

Then, abruptly, Miss Betsy closed the organ and turned to Margaret. She began to speak without looking at the girl.

"I've watched you. You aren't a fool, like everyone else. But you still have some foolishness. Folks like you, and like I was, think it's something superior to make long and romantic faces at the moon, and sigh deeply. It isn't superior, and it isn't very bright. And sometimes, when you get to the place where you realize you haven't been very bright, it's too late. Folks won't let you forget; they keep on acting as though you hadn't realized what a fool you had been; they won't believe you realize at last. And the worse part of it is that even if they'd let you alone, you'd never forget, either. You'd never forget how much of life you had lost during that time, and how you'll never regain it. And then, when folks won't let you forget, you'll hate 'em; and finally, you hate everything."

Was she trying to tell Margaret that she had been a fool not to have followed her real desire and gone off with Ralph? But how could she have known about Ralph anyway? It was very confusing. During these bewildered thoughts Margaret gazed at Miss Betsy earnestly. She felt that the older woman could tell her something if she would.

"I don't know what you mean," she said finally. "In what way am I being a fool?"

The pale gray eyes behind the spectacles looked hot and painful.

"Then, I see you haven't found out. Perhaps it won't come sudden, and you'll get over it, like getting over typhoid, slow and long, but sure. And you'll be none the worse. But, if your sickness goes on making you see things that don't exist, like a person in a fever, and then you wake up, you're going to hate yourself for a long time. If you want to be a fool, don't let anyone guess it! That's the trouble with most of us; we call the whole world to come out and watch us make fools of ourselves! You must keep it a secret!"

Margaret looked at her with quick fear and shrinking. Why, the woman was crazy! The hotness in the sunken gray eyes had turned to flame; her mouth twisted from side to side, convulsively, and the cords in her thin throat struggled with vehemence. She leaned so closely to Margaret that the girl could feel gusts of her hot breath in her face, and she involuntarily recoiled a step, glancing fearfully for a moment over her shoulder at the closed door.

Miss Betsy drew her handkerchief swiftly, almost furtively, over her lips. Then she looked at the piece of linen absently. She seemed to have forgotten Margaret; her face was entirely composed.

Then a door opened and slammed, and John's voice shouted in the dining room "Maggie! Where the devil are you?"

Margaret drew a deep breath. She had the feeling that she had been wandering in a crooked underground cavern, had turned a corner, seen sunlight, and heard a human shout close at hand. She ran to the door, opened it, called an answer in a ringing voice. Then she glanced back at Miss Betsy.

She was quietly turning down the wick of the lamp; a moment later she knelt and poked the fire. It blazed up, scarlet on her bony profile with its grim lips and the creases about them.

Margaret had two swift thoughts, Was her husband's aunt insane? Was she a friend or an enemy?

She went out into the dim hallway. John was waiting for her, puzzled and a little impatient. He came forward and seized her arm.

"Why'd you run off, Mag?"

"I wondered about your aunt, John. She wasn't over to the barn; I came back to see about her."

John raised his eyebrows.

"Aunt Betsy? Why, she never goes no place, dancin' least of all."

His expression of surprise lingered. His aunt had always been there in the background of his life, silent and efficient, but this was the first time that he thought of her as a human being. He found the idea novel.

"I kin see her dancin'!" he laughed. Margaret bit her lip, and her brows drew together.

"It isn't dancing, John. It's—something else. You never speak about her; she might just as well be stock."

John grinned. "There are some that think wimin folks is stock, Mag, belongin' to the man that owns them. Wimin folks, cattle, sheep, all the same. You, you're different, and I— But, Mag, this ain't the time for such talk! Let's be gettin' back to the music."

Margaret stared at him blankly, but she did not see him. She saw the dignity of Betsy Hobart's gaunt figure, the flaming gray eyes, the emaciated but beautifully formed hands. And then, her gaze focusing, she saw John, tall, proud, grasping at life with both hands. So there were men who considered they owned their women folks, owned their women as they owned their cows! Earthy, insensitive men like John . . .

"Come on, let's get out of here, back to the barn," John said impatiently, bursting into her thoughts with power and abruptness. He put his arms about her, nudged back her head with the side of his cheek, and kissed her long and slowly on the lips. For one blinding moment she saw Ralph's face, his wounded eyes. She struggled, and then her will dissolved, was swallowed up in a languor of inexplicable desire. Ralph's face died away.

Chapter Ten

THERE WERE THREE VASES in the druggist's window, green, yellow and red, filled with translucent and motionless liquid. Ralph Blodgett stood before the window and gazed at them, sinking deep into their color as into a sea. He shivered in the chill wind of the early November day and thought bitterly of his long ride from Whitmore to Williamsburg, how aglow he had been, how he had looked about him with bemused and smiling eyes. It was not until, at dawn, when he arrived at the deserted depot in Williamsburg that a feeling of lostness began to creep over him. He had stood in the waiting room, his bag beside him, and wondered what to do next. The room was empty; in the distance was the loud thunder of passing freight trains, the hollow echoing of disconnected sounds.

"Anythin' I can do for you, son?" called the stationmaster through the grating of the ticket window.

"I'm a stranger in town," said Ralph, hope in his voice. He looked at the older man eagerly. "I'm not quite sure where to go."

"Where you from?"

"Whitmore. I just came in."

"Well, it's most mornin'. I 'spect what you'd like is a boardinghouse, or hotel. Got any money?"

"Oh, yes," replied Ralph confidently.

"Well, I 'spect you ain't got so much that you can stand a hotel. Good roomin' house, good plain grub, that's what you want. Wait a minute."

He disappeared from behind the grating. A moment later he could be heard shouting into the baggage room. "Bob! Hey you, Bob!" Then a ruddy Swede with tremendous shoulders emerged.

"Got a young fellow in there," said the stationmaster, jerking his bald head toward the waiting room. "No folks or anybody in town. Looks like he ain't got too much cash. Whyn't you take him down to a boardin' house and get him settled?"

"You say, boss," replied Bob, touching his forehead.

The boardinghouse was filthy, bare and dismal. For four dollars a week, the slatternly landlady offered a room and two meals a day, Sunday dinner twenty-five cents extra. She catered to mill laborers and dray drivers, and when they were home it was like a barracks full of ribald and quarrelsome giants.

Ralph was lost in all this and his only sanctuary was his hall bedroom. And when that was unbearable he fled from his room to the streets, full of traffic, crowds, and icy November winds. Days went by like this, as he wandered aimlessly through the streets. He was jostled, cursed at, as he stood directly in the streams of traffic, looking about him with lost eyes.

He had realized from the first that if he were to remain in Williamsburg he would have to have a job. But he was too proud to face being rejected by inferior men, as inwardly he knew he would be. Nevertheless he had to face it, for his funds were running dangerously low, so one morning he left the house early, thinking of Margaret and determined to find work. That night he returned, tired and utterly beaten. But fear of being less a man than others gave him courage, so he went on like this day after day. He had to drive himself to leave the house, and as his money shrank, so grew his despair.

He thought once of his poetry, but he shrank at the image of alien eyes reading the lines that Margaret had loved. He could deceive her, but not himself.

It was on the fourteenth day after his arrival in Williamsburg that he stood before the druggist's window and suddenly realized, in a flash of maturity, that he and Margaret had been fools.

Ralph had never known that there were so many bewildering fields of labor in the world. Each morning he picked up a discarded newspaper in the reeking dining room and carefully looked over the advertisements for help. There were requests for such exotic creatures as bushelmen, toolmakers, assemblers, and diemakers. He wondered what they were, listlessly.

Then, one day he read an advertisement for a copy boy in the office of the Williamsburg Courier. He did not have the vaguest conception of what a copy boy was, but he knew that he filled the requirements of at least one year of high school and a neat hand. He brushed his thin coat, polished his boots, and set forth.

The offices of the Williamsburg Courier were large, urbane, and warm. Ralph's old shyness returned as he asked for the city editor. The city editor was also owner of the newspaper, but even though Ralph's eye dimly noted the name, Alfred Holbrooks, lettered upon a closed door, it did not register with any significance in his mind. He knocked gently, was shouted to from behind the door, and entered.

There were four men at desks in the room, wearing green eyeshades; they worked in their shirtsleeves and chewed tobacco. There was a warm and incredible disorder in this room, much more heartening than the neatness of the outer offices. Under glaring and spluttering gas lights spittoons glittered; at the windows the November sleet lowered and whistled. Each man leaned over his desk, rapidly writing, actively spitting, grunting, tossing paper into overflowing baskets.

The city editor was a bluff, gigantic man who ran to flabbiness instead of muscle. He was chewing a cigar, his red forehead wrinkling under a green eyeshade. The gaslights flared down on a round pink skull incredibly bald, and rolls of hard fat at the base of the brain.

As Ralph entered, he glanced up inquiringly. "Yes?" he asked.

"You— You advertised for a copy boy." Ralph straightened and tried to look winning.

"What makes you think you'd make a good copy boy?"

"Well, I've got a good education and can write neatly. and—"

"And—what else?"

"I need the job," replied Ralph with the simplicity of despair.

Holbrooks grunted. "That's as good a reason as any. Where you from?"

Ralph breathed deeply. "Whitmore township."

Holbrooks took the cigar from his mouth.

"Whitmore township? Say, you wouldn't happen to know my half-brother, Seth Holbrooks, would you?"

"Oh, yes!" Ralph said quickly, feeling confidence return. "They don't live far from my folks! Yes, I know Seth Holbrooks well!"

"You do, eh? What's your name?"

"Ralph Blodgett."

"Blodgett, eh? Say, then, you must be Susie Blodgett's boy. Well, I'll be damned! Your great-grandpap and my grandpap were first cousins! Say, I was raised in that country! Left it, though, before your time; thirty years ago. Just a shaver myself, looking for a job in town after Dad died. I ain't been back there since I left. Say, my daughter, Lydia, was just down there on a visit. Did you see her?"

Ralph had a hazy recollection of pink dimples, chestnut curls, and tiny white hands.

"Of course, I remember Lydia! She came to see my mother one day. It seems to me that I heard she was going to marry Johnny Hobart. Do you know Johnny Hobart? He's the squire, and the richest man in that country."

"John Hobart? I remember his dad, though. Mean as hell and closer than his skin. Yes, Lydia did mention young John. Said something in one letter about him being interested in her, and being very rich and big as a bull. I was going down there to see for myself when she wrote she had given him a no answer, after all. Seems she said something about him getting in a huff and marrying some other girl down there."

Holbrooks' chair creaked as he pulled his massive bulk upright and returned to business. His face sharpened.

"So, you need a job, eh? Know how much we pay a copy boy? Seven dollars a week. Hours from seven in the morning to six or more at night. How old are you, anyway? Around twenty? Um. Not much money for a man of that age. You don't know nothing about what's wanted, too. You couldn't live on that."

Ralph calculated rapidly. Four dollars for board and room—"Yes, I could!" he cried eagerly. "It's a start, anyway, Mr. Holbrooks. I can do the work, and I'll do it well. You won't be sorry if you give me the job."

Holbrooks shrugged.

"All right, then. It's yours. Seven in the morning."

"Thank you, Mr. Holbrooks!" Ralph said quickly. He could hardly believe his luck. "Thank you! I'll be here in the morning! This means a great deal to me—"

"All right, all right. Now, get out, I'm busy!"

Ralph's hand was already on the door when it burst open and Lydia Holbrooks, radiant in sealskin jacket and cloque, bounced into the room. Her chestnut curls rioted about her pink cheeks; her little hands were hidden in a small round muff. She collided with Ralph and recoiled.

"Oh! Oh, dear!" Her muff dropped to the floor; he picked it up and gave it to her gravely. She looked at him curiously, as she looked at all young men, and then her smile faded and a startled look came into her eyes.

"Why! Why, it's Mr. Blodgett! What on earth are you doing here?"

Ralph could smile now.

"I'm going to work for your father, Miss Lydia."

Her eyes leaped beyond him to her father, who was grinning at her with fondness. Her mouth fell open in wonder, and then, as she looked at Ralph again, something hard passed over her face.

"Oh," she said, with sudden and hypocritical gravity. "I see. Oh. I'm so sorry, Mr. Blodgett, about—everything."

"Why—what do you mean?" asked Ralph, puzzled.

"Why, what else but Maggie Hamilton? Of course, that's why you left home, after the way she treated you."

Ralph went a little white; a premonition clutched him.

"I don't know what you mean, Miss Lydia." He tried to look merely curious. "Margaret and I are going to be married just as soon as I can send for her. I left home a few weeks ago, so I could make a place for her—"

An expression of shock passed over Lydia's face. Then her eyes widened. It was evident to her that Ralph knew nothing as yet. She let her lip quiver slightly, and walked slowly to her father's desk.

"Oh, Papa, I can't tell him! It's too horrible!"

"Tell me," Ralph whispered, coming slowly back to the desk. "Please tell me."

"Oh, Mr. Blodgett, that I should be the one to tell you! But didn't you know that Maggie Hamilton married Mr. John Hobart over two weeks ago? I attended their wedding. And she did look so funny, in a queer gown, in the church—"

"I don't believe it!" Ralph cried harshly. "I don't believe it! It was someone else! You only saw Margaret once!"

"I tell you I'm not mistaken!" Lydia snapped. "I was at the wedding. And I did too see her more than once. We all called on her and her mother just before the wedding! In their horrible, dirty, filthy little hut!"

Ralph's heart turned over; there was an enormous sickness in him. He sat down slowly and continued to stare at Lydia. His lips moved but no sound came from them.

"Well, now, that's too bad, Ralph, my boy," Holbrooks said sympathetically. "Just when you get a job, too! Well, that's women for you; you can't trust them. Just as soon as you're out of sight, they're up to their tricks."

But Ralph did not hear him. He still stared at Lydia but now he did not see her. Then he put a hand over his eyes.

Lydia had paled a little; she touched Ralph's shoulder timidly.

"I'm sorry," she whispered.

Chapter Eleven

"Yes, ma'am," said Susie Blodgett, as she arrogantly refolded Ralph's letter. "That's what he says; he's got a good job with Miss Lydia's father. Newspaper work. He likes it fine. He'll go far, my boy. Why, Miss Lydia's sweet as pie to him. Sees him often in her Pa's office, and gossips with him whenever she can. She's a real lady, Miss Lydia." She looked at Margaret with venom.

Margaret sat opposite, pale and quiet, in violet silk and new fur jacket. On her beaver hat nodded several plumes, and she wore furred boots. Outside waited her buggy with its big black horse and silvered harness.

It was just two days before Christmas; a thick gray snow was falling silently over the fields and the black hills, and a sharp wind moaned down the chimney. The fire crackled and leapt and gleamed on the old horsehair furniture of Susan Blodgett's parlor.

"Does—does Ralph know I am married?" asked Margaret in a low voice. "Does he say anything about me?" She thought, It's going the way we always planned, Ralph and I, only now I belong to John.

Susan squinted as though trying to remember.

"No, don't remember that he did. Wal, let me see." She unfolded the letter again, mouthed the words inaudibly. "Oh, yes, right here, at the bottom, he does."

She read, " 'Heard from Miss Lydia some time ago that Margaret married John Hobart. Tell her when you see her that I hope she will be very happy.' That's all."

Margaret's lips seemed to grow ashen. She looked steadily at the fire. She had come today to this house, as she had done several times in the last few weeks, merely to hear news of Ralph. A week ago, according to his mother, his first letter had arrived.

87

Susan Blodgett regarded her niece with malicious dislike.

"Mark my words, my boy'll amount to somethin'. You'll see."

"Yes, of course he will," replied Margaret gently, still without looking at her aunt. "It was the best thing in the world for Ralph to leave the country."

Susan bridled. "You can bet your bottom dollar on that!" she shrilled. "If he'd a stayed here he might've got tangled up with some iggerent gal hereabouts and married her! And that would have been the last of him!"

Margaret raised her muff and rubbed her cheek with it, as though her thoughts were far away. She was thinking intensely of Ralph. Beyond the curtness of the few words in his letter to his mother, she read his shock, his despair at his cousin's treachery, and his repudiation of her.

She had a sensation that inevitability had taken hold of her, that everything was done, that there would never be anything more. The door between herself and Ralph had closed for all time; it would never open again. Somehow, she had never thought of that. Mingled with her sadness was a hopeless pain.

She was about to ask her aunt for his address, but she stopped. Explanations were useless. He would just have to go on believing what he wanted to believe. She would have to get what news she could of him through his mother, whom she suspected would give her as little as possible.

She rose with a rustle of silk; against the richness of her furs her face was still calm and pale, under the brim of her hat her eyes were unreadable.

"It's getting late, Aunt Susie. I'd best be going."

It was the first snow of the season, wet and clinging. When it was packed down, and freezing, Margaret thought, she would use a sleigh. Every farmhouse that she passed was shrouded and huddled, a mere blur of smoke hanging over its eaves, the windows bleak. She shivered in her furs. The harness jingled, but the horse's hoofs made no sound on the cushioned road.

As she drove along, Margaret had a weird feeling that

the old Margaret Hamilton was dead, that she had mysteriously bequeathed to a stranger her memories. This woman in this buggy, comfortable, furclad, was that stranger. Surely it was only a memory of weariness and grief that she was suffering; between herself and poignancy was a wall.

I'm useless; I'm inadequate. I'm not living at all, she thought.

It was almost dark when she sighted the row of pointed poplars that stood near the "old house." Every window was dark except for a dim light in the kitchen, where the hired girl was getting supper. But from the house came a prolonged murmur of organ music. Margaret shivered. She knew now that Miss Betsy was her enemy, that in some strange and inexplicable way she had lost a friendship, that it had died before it had hardly begun.

The "new house" was brightly warm and reassuring in the night. Voices, borne clearly on the silence, came from the barn, John's voice and those of his half-dozen hired men. She would have time to slip in before he came to the house. She drove to the separate barn where the horses were kept, and was pleased to find a youth there, feeding the other horses. She spoke to him brightly, though he did not reply. She knew that she was not popular with the help, that they feared her, though she was too indifferent to wonder why. She leaped from the buggy, and then ran swiftly to the house.

Inside all was warm fires, comfort, and even luxury. The new walnut furniture gleamed; the gaily flowered walls were covered with bright pictures; brass glimmered everywhere. John had spared no expense in making himself as pleasant a home as possible. The house, square and solid, was as he had wanted it.

He had told Margaret that she was to be a lady. So two hired girls lived in the house, and Margaret had nothing much to do. She could sew if she wanted to, but he desired her only to look after her household, to dress herself richly and soberly, to sit at his table and delight his eyes. This revolutionary manner of living had scandalized the countryfolk, who believed that women

were made for labor, for the kitchen, and for the bedroom.

"So he's made Maggie Hamilton a lady!" they jeered.
"Wal, Johnny Hobart will soon find out he can't make a
silk purse out of a sow's ear!"

As "Pete Hamilton's zany" Margaret has always been a
refreshing local joke, as were all the Hamiltons. But it
had been indulgent ridicule, even affectionate occasionally. Now the ridicule remained, but grown harder, full
of envy and obscure indignation.

Margaret had never been hated before, except by her
mother and her aunt Susan; now almost everyone hated
her, would have been delighted at any disaster that might
strike at her.

She was at first amused by the hatred, then indifferent.
The farm women came to her new house to admire, to
stare. They clucked obsequiously to Margaret, listened
attentively when she spoke. But out of the corner of her
eye she saw their glances at each other, the poisonous
smiles, the lightning of hate in their watchful eyes. Once
she said to herself, I'm Margot Hamilton's great-granddaughter. She was Lady Margot of London, of the great-
est nation on the earth. Who are these descendants of
convicts, of bondsmen and bondswomen, of farmers?
And hated herself that she could debase herself by thinking of them. Her only consolation was that John knew
nothing of this universal hatred. In his presence, the
hatred was silent; he was too powerful, he held too many
mortgages.

He was not displeased that Margaret paid few visits
to their neighbors, that her only friend was old Mis'
Holbrooks, that his house was not "tracked up by wom-
en-folk." He and Margaret went to church with Miss
Betsy on Sunday, sat together decorously, left in a
compact body, nodding and smiling distantly to ac-
quaintances. Margaret and his aunt never attended the
"meetin's," never were present at quilting bees and
church suppers, John went to them merely to keep an eye
on the activities of his miniature kingdom. He was afraid
that if he mingled with the county people, whose farms

were his natural prey, he might relent to a basic kindness in him, and John Hobart considered sentiment a dangerous thing.

He had anticipated some trouble with Margaret about her family, but as time went on he was gratified that none of the family visited. He had a suspicion that Peter came occasionally, but as he did not see him personally, he said nothing. When his children were born he did not want them to know much about the Hamiltons, except old Margot. He already had plans which would have been grandiose in a lesser man.

Margaret ran up the white circular staircase to the huge front bedroom which she shared with John. The small fire licked at the grate, burnished the rich walnut and the silver candlesticks. She patted her hair into place, glanced at her dark features in the glass and ran downstairs again. She heard John's whistle outside and hurried into the dining room. She had barely seated herself when he entered.

"Brr-rr!" he said as he came in, shuddering strongly. "Gettin' cold as hell out. Hope there's somethin' fit to eat."

He went to the white-tiled hearth and rubbed his fingers appreciatively. The firelight glimmered on his face, revealing the harsh lines of strength and the shadows of fatigue. Margaret watched him calmly, studying the mighty breadth of shoulder, the power of hard thigh. Her face showed no expression.

"There's always something fit to eat," she said equably.

"Huh. Wonder if there is, with you sashayin' all over the county. Where you been today? Thought I wouldn't see you run in, didn't you?"

He came to the table, eying her without kindness. There was resentment in his expression, an old resentment which had been born the day after their marriage.

"I wasn't trying to hide," said Margaret indifferently. "Why should I?" She gestured to the girl to lay the platter of ham in a certain position. "I went to see my aunt, that's all."

"Your aunt!" he barked, and the hired girl recoiled.

"Goin' there to hear news of that weakling cousin of yours, weren't you!"

Margaret was silent. She passed the bowl of winter cabbage to John. He helped himself with a hand unsteady with anger. The girl listened avidly.

"If you was so damn crazy about Ralph Blodgett, whyn't you marry him 'stead of me?" he continued. The old bewildered resentment found voice at last. "Ever since we been married I've felt somethin'. Somethin' hidin' back in your mind. And it's Ralph, isn't it?"

"Ralph is my cousin; I've known him all my life. Naturally, I want to know what he's doing in town," replied Margaret very quietly. She was sickened; this would be all over the county tomorrow, whispered among her gleeful enemies. "If I'd wanted to marry him instead of you, I could have done it. You have no right to say such things to me."

"No right! That's fine talk from a wife!" John glared at her; behind his rage was his almost pathetic desire to find his way back. She saw it and smiled a little, indulgently.

"He's got a job with the father of Lydia Holbrooks; you remember, the girl who tried so hard to marry you," she said lightly.

Despite himself, John grinned. He became interested. "He did, eh? Bet he's runnin' errands. Well, I ain't interested." He thrust a huge slice of ham into his mouth. "Know what I did today? Two things. Took a mortgage out on Ezra King's farm; two thousand dollars! And bought that prize bull they was showin' at the Fair last summer, bought it for a song! Now we'll have some real cattle!"

"Is there any farm in the county you haven't taken a mortgage on?" asked Margaret, smiling.

Well pleased, his good temper returned. "Hardly any. I'll soon have this county where I want it, in the palm of my hand. Then I'll show folks hereabouts somethin' about agriculture, how farms should be run. They have to be beat over the head with newfangled methods, before they accept them. If it ain't like their fathers used to do it, then it's wrong. Well, I'll get them so they'll have to listen to John Hobart, and then we'll make this countryside somethin' to see."

His smile broadened. He felt that the air had cleared between them. He beamed on her appreciatively, and she smiled in return.

"Say, Maggie! Heard somethin' good today. The railroad is thinkin' o' buying land around here, to run a branch line down to Kensington. Or maybe farther. Only way they can go is down beyond the old mill, touchin' my land. D'ye know what that means? Thousands! 'Spect it'll run along your pa's farm, too, and he'll make a sight of money. Well, we don't know about it, yet. Have to wait and see."

"Do you mean Pa might be asked to sell his farm?"

"His farm!" John snorted. "D'ye call them piddlin' little acres a farm? God Almighty! It's just a front yard! Chance of a lifetime for him; sell it for thousands. Ought to get down on his knees and pray to the Lord to make it come true."

"Pa'd never sell that farm, John. It's been in the family since Great-grandpa Sam Hamilton."

"What are you talkin' about! The whole thing ain't worth two hundred dollars. Land all wore out, full of stones and old stumps. Can't raise nothin' on it but a few pertatoes and weeds. Fences all broken down, brook all choked up. Good-for-nothin'."

"Still, Pa won't sell it. It's our land."

John was about to speak again, but his eyes suddenly narrowed as he stared at his wife.

"Say, ain't that farm your'n, Maggie? Didn't the ole girl leave it to you? By God!" His fist banged down on the table. "Then, it's mine! That's the law, Maggie, and you can't get away from it!"

Margaret looked at him, the muscles of her face rigid.

John was more excited, and somewhat angry. "Why, my land wouldn't be worth nothin' to the railroad without that strip of stony ole land. They wouldn't buy. And by God, I ain't goin' to let a lot of foolish ideas get in my way, 'bout land belongin' to the family."

Margaret tried to speak, then closed her mouth. She felt suddenly weary. "We'll see," she said at last.

They went into the sitting room where a batch of fresh newspapers awaited John. They sat down before the fire. The night wind was rising; it rushed down the chimney, scattered sparks. From the dining room came the subdued clatter of dishes. The lamps flared a little. The house basked in its richness and warmth. Margaret glanced through some of the papers idly. Her thoughts ran about like distracted small animals.

Was Ralph thinking of her tonight, thinking of her treachery? Tears rose to her eyes. All at once the house became a prison with walls of iron and stone, from which she would never escape, in which she would smother. She belonged with Ralph, helping him, talking over his work with him at night, reading his newest poem, pouring tea for the circle of cultured people who would be his friends. She looked at John, half dozing in his big chair, the newspapers sliding on his knees. Suddenly she hated him, shrank from him. His blundering attempts to approach her seemed no longer pathetic to her, but greedy.

Ralph's face·rose before her, pale and delicate. She clenched her hands in her lap. It could not be possible that she would never see him again, never talk to him, never hear that light and eager voice. The full realization of her loss swept over her, closing her throat in anguish. What had she done? Had she been mad? Unable to endure her suffering any longer, she started up. John did not stir.

She crept from the room, softly opened the door, and closed it behind her. She did not feel the rush of cold damp air through the silk of her arms. The wind leaped at her, lifted her hair, choked back her breath for a moment. She looked out into the night.

It had stopped snowing, and a pale moon scurried through ragged clouds. The whole world was white and utterly silent. She could see the black hills beyond, like a monster lying prone upon the horizon. There was dolorous dripping in the eaves from the melting snow. She looked at the sky; here and there a pointed star peered through the clouds, and then was swallowed up.

Even as she thought of Ralph, the farm smells assaulted her.

She began to cry as she stood there, with slow and catching breaths. When she went in, she did not know whether she was resigned or merely numb.

Chapter Twelve

THE APRIL RAINS had been long and chilly, and now, though they had ceased, the sun did not shine; under a sky like gloomy gray glass the world was a mist of swimming greenness. Under the sadness of the still and sunless air was a promise, a stirring.

"I declare to goodness, this here dampness gets into everythin'," said Mrs. Holbrooks to Margaret as they sat by the smoldering fire of the new house "settin' room." "Only this mornin' I tried to open Seth's chest to put away his winter socks and I had to pry the drawers loose. I always say t'aint healthy to sleep on the ground floor, but Seth likes it, and now he barks like an old dog."

Margaret knitted quietly. In the firelight her needles flashed; her face was calm and expressionless. The gray and heavy daylight flooded the room, for the saplings were not yet tall and thick enough to press their green gloom against the windows.

"How you feelin', Maggie?" went on the old woman, who was knitting, too.

"Very well."

"Can't get around much, though, can ye? Well, that's the price we pay for young uns, and sometimes I think it's too much of a price. Folks say we must feel right bad, not havin' any of our own, but I say when they're little, they tread on your toes, and when they're grown, they tread on your heart. Anyways, it's the Lord's will, either way," she added with a comfortable sigh that had no regret in it.

Margaret smiled faintly. Her hand dropped to her side and she glanced through the window. Her face changed. "Here comes Aunt Betsy. She hasn't been here but once since we moved in."

She watched Miss Betsy approaching with rigid determination across the wet brown earth. She disappeared around the side of the house, in the direction of the kitchen door. Margaret made a quick movement, coloring with annoyance. In a few moments the sitting room door opened and Betsy Hobart entered decisively. Mrs. Holbrooks looked over her glasses at the visitor.

"Well, howdy, Betsy. Ain't seen you in a month of Sundays."

Betsy stopped abruptly near the door. She frowned, her face tightening. She looked at Margaret with an expression of cold annoyance.

"I didn't know you had visitors," she said.

"Land sakes, I'm no visitor!" said Mrs. Holbrooks with a chuckle. "I'm a friend."

"Sit down, please," said Margaret, indicating a chair. But Miss Betsy, though she moved to the chair, only stood behind it, clutching the top. She glared at the girl for a moment.

"You haven't started a garden. I was just wondering if you wanted to start one. If you are, you'd better do it right away. I've got some seeds and plants I could give you."

Margaret looked at her, moved. "Thank you," she replied gently. "I haven't thought about a garden. I'd like to have one. I could bring over some of my grandmother's rose bushes. . . ."

She was enormously touched, eager to approach the older woman again. But Miss Betsy's face was still relentless.

"Always have a garden, I say," said Mrs. Holbrooks, knitting tranquilly. "It kind of brings you closer to things." She seemed not to have noticed the other woman's rudeness.

Miss Betsy glanced at her contemptuously. "Margaret, I want to say something to you."

Margaret hesitated, embarrassed. Then she left the room, followed by her husband's aunt. Once in the large dim hall outside, she waited in silence. She looked at Miss Betsy; the older woman's face had changed. Her gray lips were dry. When she spoke her voice was low, hurried, yet sharp.

"Did John tell you that he's arranging to sell old Margot's land—to the railroad? It'll go right across the graves, over old Margot's grave, and the others. Did you know that?"

Margaret stared at her blankly. "He never told me that," she whispered. She put her cold fingers swiftly to her face. "He can't do that! It's Pa's land! It's my land!"

Miss Betsy shrugged. "I didn't think he'd told you. He did say he was going to drive over to see your father about it tonight. I thought you ought to know. Now then, don't tell him I told you."

She went abruptly toward the farther door. There she paused. She glanced back at Margaret; there was a warning expression on her face. Then she went out. Margaret stood there for a moment, confused, angered, filled with panic. She went back to Mrs. Holbrooks. The old woman was standing, gathering her knitting.

"Gettin' late. Well, Maggie, I've had a nice time, settin' here talkin'. Kin you and Johnny ride over Sunday and eat dinner with us?"

"Yes. No! I don't know," replied Margaret, shaken. She pushed back her hair from her forehead that was damp. Mrs. Holbrooks did not look at her. She continued to chatter amiably as Margaret helped her into her shawls and gave her her bonnet.

"Hear that Johnny's got a mortgage on every farm in the county, 'cept ours," she chuckled. "'Spect he's plannin' for that boy you got comin' in June, Maggie." She chuckled louder. "Lots of folks hereabouts are agoin' to be disappointed that he's comin' in June. They kind of expected he'd be comin' in March or this month."

Margaret smiled mechanically. When her visitor had gone, she discovered that her hands were trembling. She sat before the fire and stared blindly at it.

After a little while, one of the hired girls, a ruddy country wench, opened the door without knocking and put her head into the room.

"You there, Mis' Hobart? Your sister Linda's out in

the kitchen. Told her to go right in here, but she wouldn't. She wants to see you."

"I'm coming." Margaret stood up. She went out into the big kitchen where the two hired girls were cooking and baking. Fifteen-year-old Linda, shabby, thin and tall in her baggy coat, her head wet with rain, stood shyly near the kitchen door.

"Hello, Linda," Margaret said gently, kissing the girl's rosy cheek.

"I kin only stay a minit," mumbled the girl defensively.

"Come into the sitting room, Linda, and talk to me. Mary," she said to one of the hired girls, "bring in some coffee and some of that cake from supper last night."

In the sitting room Margaret tried to get Linda to remove her coat, but the girl refused stubbornly. It was evident that she was uneasy in all this clean grandeur. She had never been here before. She sat on the edge of a chair, glancing resentfully about. Margaret studied her thoughtfully. In a year or two, she thought with pleased surprise, Linda would be very pretty. Her hair was thick and fine, shining with pure gold. Her bones were delicate and gracefully formed. Her eyes were large and blue, edged with thick, yellow lashes. Her nose was piquant and small, her lips full and pouting.

"I kin only stay a minit," muttered Linda again. She twisted uneasily on her chair. "Ma sent me. She said not to tell Pa."

"Well, what is it, Linda?" asked Margaret encouragingly. She wanted to be affectionate; for the first time she realized that between herself and the rest of Melinda Hamilton's children was a bitter wall of hostility. Linda was her mother's favorite; she would never be close to Margaret Hobart.

Linda shuffled her feet. "Well," she muttered. "Pa won't buy Ma any more medicine. Said she's pilled and drunk him down. So he won't buy her no more. She said she'd die without 'em. And he said go, then, and die. I'm sick alookin' at your miserable face, anyways." She glanced up at Margaret, real fright and childish grief on her face. "And so, Ma was wonderin' if you'd help her. Lend her a little money, and not tell Pa. She'll die if you don't."

Margaret studied the thin, half-starved body, the ugly shoes, the torn coat. Melinda's pills and bottles had robbed her children of decencies.

"Linda, have you gone to school much this winter?" she asked suddenly.

Linda, forgetting her shyness, looked up and stared at her sister, confused at this irrelevance.

"No, I ain't," she stammered. "Only 'bout a month. Ma's been porely all winter, though I 'spect you didn't know," she added reproachfully. "You ain't been over to see her but once, after Christmas. Ma said she didn't hold much for book learnin'. Not much use."

"Why, Linda, you can hardly read or write! It's a shame."

Linda stood up abruptly, began to fumble on her coat for buttons that were not there.

"If you don't want to lend Ma the money—" she began.

Obeying an obscure impulse, Margaret caught at the girl's hand, forced her to look at her between her flickering yellow lashes.

"Do you want me to lend her the money, Linda?" she asked with a desperate attempt to approach the child.

Linda stared, blinking. Then her face dissolved into tears. "I don't want Ma to die!" she sobbed. Margaret stood up, put her arms about the thin shoulders, which silently repulsed her.

"Then, Linda," she said gently, "I'll give her the money. She mustn't even think about returning it! I really owe it to her." She kissed the child's shrinking cheek, allowed Linda to withdraw a step from her. Her heart ached with new pain.

"Ma won't die," she said. "She's always had her pills and things. If she still wants them, she can have them. Don't cry, Linda, dear. I—I want to help you. And Linda, you'll come to see me often, won't you? I want to see you. I want to help you. The others are so little. But you are grown now. We can be such friends, together. You'll

try to love me a little, won't you, Linda?" Her voice
was infinitely pleading, gentle.

"Well, Ma's porely. She needs me. 'Spect I can't come
often. But there ain't nothin' to keep you from comin' to
see Ma, Maggie." Her sliding eye fixed itself curiously
on Margaret's swollen body. Margaret shrank from that
glance; it seemed impure, sniggering. She ached again for
the child.

"I'll come," she said. "I'll really come, Linda. I just
didn't think anyone wanted me." She felt defensive.
"Well, here's your coffee and cake," she said as Mary
entered with a tray.

"I'm not hungry," said Linda with renewed hostility.

Mary laid the tray on the table and withdrew, her
nose high.

"But you must eat it. You've got a long walk home.
And while you eat it, I'll go upstairs for my purse. Sit
down, Linda. See, it's real nice cake and good hot coffee.
Sit down here, right by the fire, and dry yourself."

The girl obeyed unwillingly.

Margaret went heavily upstairs, dragging legs that
seemed weighted with lead. She went to her room and
counted out three big silver dollars, went to her wardrobe, withdrew a nearly new warm coat and two woolen
dresses. She wrapped up the garments in a bright red
shawl and then went downstairs again. Linda had eaten
the cake, every crumb, and had drunk the coffee. She
seemed ashamed and angry as Margaret entered, and
pushed the dishes roughly from her. Margaret began to
speak cheerfully.

"Here's three dollars, Linda. And here's a nice shawl
for Ma. And in the shawl's a nice coat for you and two
dresses. Almost new. You'll like them."

Linda stared at the garments. "We don't want your
ole cast-off things. We ain't beggars," she said rudely. But
her blue eyes were fixed longingly on the bundle.

"Beggars?" repeated Margaret, smiling. "Are my
mother and sister beggars if they take something I can
give them? Here, child, put the coat on. There, it fits
beautifully! How warm it seems, with that little high fur

collar. Ma will like the shawl; it's always cold at home."

The dark-brown fur heightened the milky-whiteness of Linda's flesh, brightened the blue eyes, gave the childish form a certain regality which Margaret's possessed. She's beautiful, thought Margaret wistfully. I've got to do something for Linda.

The girl left soon, listening to Margaret's gentle advice and tenderness with a faint smile of malice. Margaret watched her go, sighing.

It was only about half-past three when John came in, shaking his hat free of clinging raindrops, stamping and shouting.

"There you are, old girl! Feelin' all right? That's fine. Goin' to give me a kiss?"

He swept Margaret up from her chair into the circle of his arms, kissed her thoroughly. She made a small mechanical gesture of repulsion, but, despite herself, the warm security that was John flooded her, and she relaxed. She dropped her hand on his shoulder, closing her eyes. If only he would hold me like this all the time, I would never think of anything else, she thought. But when he released her and she looked up into the glowing face, she felt a physical withdrawal, a sense of disorientation. This man was a stranger; he had no right to her body. They had nothing to say to each other.

"Fourteen cows calved today and yesterday," he said with satisfaction as he sat down before the fire. " 'Spect ten more to calve tomorrow or the next day. First thing you know, we'll have the best stock farm in the whole state! Everythin's comin' along fine. Elmer Cannon'd better be ready with his mortgage money in June, or I'll have another nice strip of bottom land! Time and again I've tried to show him how to get the most from his place, but he's plain shiftless."

"He's got ten children," said Margaret.

"Eh? Ten young uns? Was I their dad?" He chuckled. "What the hell does he want with ten, anyway? If he spent less time in bed and more down in his fields he'd be able to take care of things like mortgages and such. I can't be Santa Claus and support a lot of shiftless kids."

Margaret's listless face became animated. "Something might be done about that, John. All these children, and no place for them. Like—like Ma and Pa. Linda was here a while ago, and she's getting so pretty. But she never goes to school because Ma's poorly. She's had ten children. And Linda, I suppose, will marry someone like herself, and that'll be the end of her."

John scowled. "Well, what do you want me to do? Start a county farm 'specially to house the overflow of brats?" He looked thoughtful. "Might not be a bad idea. Anyway, Linda's nearly growed now. Why can't the gal hire herself out?"

"Your wife's sister working in someone's kitchen?" suggested Margaret shrewdly. John pulled at his lower lip, frowning. Then, to Margaret's surprise, his scowl faded and his face assumed a certain blandness.

"Well, who knows? Perhaps your Pa'll get some money, somehow, and do somethin' for his young uns." He stood up, stretching his arms, not meeting her eye. "I think I'll run down to his place and talk to him a spell. One of the men said he saw Pete goin' home a while ago. 'Spect there's nothin' much doin' at the forge."

Margaret stood up, too. She tried to speak casually. "I'll go with you. Linda was saying Ma's sick, and I ought to see her. Besides, Dr. Webster said last week that I should get out as much as possible."

John shook his head. "No, ma'am, you ain't ridin' over those roads in any buggy with me. Only a couple of months now and I ain't takin' chances. I'm countin' on that boy of mine."

Margaret laid her hand on his arm, smiled up at him cajolingly. "John, I'm no city lady. I'm used to bad roads. I'm as strong as an ox. I want to see Ma. I don't want you to leave me here alone. Please take me; I'm lonesome."

John was about to refuse again, but a thought struck him. Might as well get everything over at once, he thought, and no more shilly-shallying. If I drive slow maybe it won't hurt her. He smiled indulgently.

"Come on, then. Wrap up warm. Weather's treacherous yet. Here, give me another kiss, first."

They drove under dripping green canopies of trees over a road like a muddy river. On each side stretched fields that looked like wet gray corduroy, lonely, running and desolate. Moisture dripped on the roof of the buggy; brown water splashed onto the floor. John smoked his pipe, and so heavy was the damp air that the smoke refused to leave the interior of the buggy and filled it with acrid fog. Both husband and wife were unusually silent. Though John removed his pipe once or twice and seemed about to say something, he always replaced it and stared glumly before him. They drove very slowly.

The little Hamilton shack seemed extraordinarily desolate, its eaves drifting with a fog of smoke. The wails of children could be heard from within, and the angry roar of Peter's voice.

As John hitched his horse to a post, the door opened and Peter himself stamped out, shouting. He gaped with surprise at the sight of his visitors, then his huge and hairy face lighted with pleasure. He came to them boisterously, kissed Margaret smartly, and insisted on shaking John's hand. Nevertheless, there was constraint between the two men.

Margaret held her velvet skirts high to avoid the gritty floors. Melinda was lying on a cot at one side of the stove, huddled beneath dirty quilts, while the children swarmed about her. Linda was preparing biscuits, her thin young arms white with flour. Margaret glanced about, sickened. Had she actually spent nineteen years in such a place? She shivered even while she went to her mother.

Melinda was really ill this time. Her face was drawn, her white lips blistered and dry, her gray plaits sprawled over the wrinkled sheet. She watched Margaret's approach, and, despite her illness, her old malevolence sprang into her sunken eyes.

"So you fin'ly decided to come to visit your pore relations, Maggie?"

"Ma! You're sick!"

"Much you care, Maggie, with your fine new clothes and fine new house and fine new husband!" She cast a vicious look at John, who was now entering with Peter just behind him.

John drew in a breath of the rank air. "Whew!" he cried. "I don't hold much with this new fangled idea of lots of fresh air, but this place would be better if you'd open a window! How're you, Ma?" He loomed in the place like an ox in a small stable.

Melinda began to whimper.

"Oh, shut up!" said Peter irritably. "John and Maggie didn't come to hear you grunt! Set down, John. Set down, Maggie. 'Spect you oughtn't be on your feet much, eh?"

Melinda became weakly hysterical. "Yes, Pete Hamilton, you can make a fuss of 'em, and they never comin' near the place to see if we be dead or alive, or starvin', or anythin', for months! You never did have no more character than a kicked dog!"

John shrugged good-naturedly. "Never mind, Pete. See here, Ma, didn't you get them hams and spuds and cabbages I sent you? Sure, you did! Well, that means you ain't starved none. And how about that cow I gave you when your own died on you? Still givin' milk, eh? And them sacks of flour and sides of bacon? Well, now! And didn't I give Pete here thirty dollars at Christmas to help pay his taxes and make things easy for you?"

Pete glowered. "Oh, she's allus bellyachin'. Give her the world and she'd ask you for the sky. Shet up, now, Melindy." He jerked his head toward the "settin' room." "Come on in there, John. Kin see you got somethin' on your mind. Maggie can stay here with her ma and listen to her gruntin's."

Margaret watched the door close behind the men, then hastily withdrew her leather purse from her muff. She emptied it on the table near her mother's bed. Ten round silver dollars. Melinda's sharp and wizened face changed; her hot hand slipped over the money and put it under her pillow. None of the children saw it.

"I'll send Dr. Webster over tomorrow, Ma," said Margaret. Then, removing her coat and throwing it over a chair, she opened the door and went into the "settin' room." John was standing by the smoldering wood fire, filling his pipe. Peter was smoking comfortably as he rocked in one of the shabby chairs. He had removed his boots and was stretching his toes out to the blaze. John turned and frowned as Margaret entered.

"Why don't you stay with your ma?"

"Because I have an idea this concerns me, too."

"Eh?" said Peter, sitting upright, and looking sharply from husband to wife. "What's all this, anyway?"

John gestured with annoyance. "Oh, all right! All right! Wimin pokin' their noses into others' business! Pete," turning abruptly to his father-in-law, "has anybody asked you to sell your farm to the railroad?"

"Eh? Railroad? Um. Wal, yes, now that you speak of it, they did. Last winter. Some feller from Williamsburg dickered awhile, but I said, 'No, sir. I ain't sellin' this here ole farm. No, sir. It's mine. Run your ole steam cars over some other folks' farm, not mine!'"

John smiled indulgently. "Say, you're bein' chuckleheaded, Pete! Know how much they want to give you? Two thousand! Two thousand dollars for this worthless strip of land. Why, it ain't worth two hundred dollars! Let me handle this for you. Say! I just took over a farm in Banford township. Worth four thousand if it's worth a cent. One hundred and fifty acres. Five cows, three horses, two hundred chickens, good well, good house, fine barn and outbuildings, and seventy-five acres of it, the best bottom land I ever saw. I'll let you have it for the two thousand! What do you say?"

He beamed from father to daughter with a proud consciousness of his own magnanimity. Peter shook his head.

"No, sir, Johnny! This here land's belonged to the Hamiltons for nigh onto a hunnerd years. Nearly. Why, old Margot's buried right where the railroad'd run, and so's old great-grandpa Sam Hamilton, and most of their young uns. They'd run their damn rails right over their graves. 'Sides, this is my land. It's part of me, Johnny. Money never did seem more important, someways, than the place where you belong, and where your folks died and got buried. I git along. And when I'm dead, Johnny, and you're dead, it won't make no difference to us if we left money in the bank and good acres, or jest had a good time, smokin' and gassin', like me."

John controlled himself with an effort. "That don't make sense, Pete. You got a family. Young uns growin' up wild, without no schoolin'. Why, that gal of yours, Linda, ought to have a chanc't. Pretty gal. If you had a good farm, she'd git herself a good husband. Look at this damn' place! Git yourself somethin' decent, and you'll be able to have your young uns look like somebody instead of heathen."

"Say," drawled Peter. His black eyes narrowed. "Why you so all-fired set on me sellin' out? Where do you come in on this?"

John chuckled good humoredly. He looked at Peter frankly. "Well, tell you the truth, Pete, they want to buy that southeast strip of mine, too. It's longer'n your'n, and then, there's the hill they want to tunnel. Run out through the other side, to your wife's sister's place. 'Spect they'll be askin' her to sell, too, if they get your land. T'ain't fair, Pete, to keep me and Susie Blodgett from turnin' a penny. And they won't buy ours without your'n."

Peter sat back into his chair and smoked for a few moments. "So that's how it is," he said slowly. Then he shook his head. "No, sir! I ain't sellin'. And that's my last word." He slapped the arm of his chair and rose.

Before John could answer, the door opened and Melinda, wrapped in a blanket, stood in the doorway. Her straggling hair fell over her shoulders; fever and rage burned in her eyes. Margaret went to her involuntarily, put her arm about her mother. But the woman did not notice her; she was glaring at Peter with frenzied hatred.

"I heard, Peter Hamilton! I heard! And you'll keep your fam'ly and me stuck on this no-account place just because your ole grandma's buried here! And we could live on a fine farm, with a good house and stock and good water, and you'd keep us here on this turrible place out of plumb stubbornness, jest because you're afraid of a little work! That's all bothers you, Peter Hamilton! You allus was shiftless!"

John's face smoothed into a gratified smile.

"Well, that's how it is, Ma. That's what I been tellin' Pete. He ain't got no right keepin' his woman and his kids on this place, when he's got a chance to improve himself. I been tellin' him—"

"You mean, damn you, you been tellin' him to help you get a few measly dollars!" shouted Peter, shaking his fist under John's nose. "Much you care what becomes of us! Well, here's my last word—I ain't sellin'! And you can't make me sell! And no one's goin' to make me let the steam cars run over old Margot's grave!" He turned to the silent Margaret. "Maggie! You ain't said a word. Come now, do you want me to sell out ole Margot's grave and the Hamilton's land? My ole grandma wuz mighty good to you; loved you better'n anybody. Think she'd like you to do that?"

Margaret turned frankly to her husband and her father. "Yes, Pa, she'd like us to do that," she said quietly. Peter's mouth fell open with astonishment; John broke out into a surprised and affectionate smile. "Yes, she'd like us to do that, Pa. She'd say, 'Don't be fools. My old body isn't worth your life. Go on, and live.' That's what she'd say. But," she added slowly, "that's not what we think. And we, being alive, have the right to what we feel. We couldn't bear to have the graves run over and mangled, and their markings gone. We have the right to those graves, more than the people in them have. We are Hamiltons; they are our people. We can't consider what they'd think or do. We must do what we want to. We are living; they are only dead."

Peter looked at his daughter soberly, almost respectfully.

But John burst out, enraged, "What's all this damn talk about the livin' and the dead? That don't enter into it. Hard cash is enterin' in it. And that's what life is, my girl! Hard cash. On one side you got those damn silly graves, and on the other, hard cash. That's all. And you'd make your pore Ma here, and that sister of yours, Linda, 'bout which you was whinin' this evenin', and all the other kids, live on here, half starvin' and puny, without no chanc't to live. Just for graves! God, you make me sick!"

Melinda, recovering from her stupefaction, struck her daughter a feeble blow in the chest.

"You allus stood with your Pa, Maggie! A bad, no-account, shiftless gal, that you are! You ain't got no heart in you; you ain't got no sense. You're just like your Pa. You want me to die; you want those pore young uns to die, so you won't be 'shamed of us any more, now you got a fine house and a fine husband! You want to keep us here, then play the grand lady and give us a measly dollar whenever you think of it, and some of your ole rags! I don't want 'em! I don't want nothin' you got! I'll spit on them, like this!" and she spat fully into Margaret's face.

"Here, here!" said John, forgetting for a moment his quarrel with Peter. "Don't you do that to my wife! Maggie, come over here, near me!"

He seized Margaret's arm and dragged her across the room. Peter laid his mighty hands on his wife's frail shoulders and thrust her from the room, dropping the old wooden bar into place behind her. On the other side of the door Melinda beat with her fists, shrieking feebly.

John resumed the argument where it had left off. But now his voice was quiet and hard.

"All right, then. You make me do what I didn't want to do. Ole Margot left this land to Maggie, here. It's her'n. And she bein' my wife, it's mine. I'll sell it over your head. That's my final word. Think it over. You'll sell the land like a gentleman to the railroad, or I'll sell it. That's the law. Come on, Maggie."

"You can't do that, John!" cried Margaret. "I won't let you do that!"

"You'll have nothin' to say 'bout it, my fine lady," said John between his teeth. She could not resist his grasp; he propelled her as if she were a child. She protested without result and stumbled over her own feet. In the kitchen Melinda had sunk upon her bed. Linda shot a malicious glance at her sister; the children were sober and frightened, standing near their mother's bed. John thrust Margaret's arms into her coat; he caught up her muff and dragged her firmly to the door. Peter followed them into the kitchen.

"Go on, Johnny Hobart," he said in a deadly voice. "Go on, it don't matter. But there's a law besides hard cash, Johnny Hobart."

"Yes? And what is that law, Pete?"

He thrust Margaret out into the cold wetness of the April night. He half carried, half dragged her, with a sort of rough tenderness, to the buggy. He swung her carefully to her seat, where she collapsed, sobbing silently. They drove away and John began to hum good-naturedly. Once or twice he chuckled. Then at last he put his big arm about his wife, tilted up her face with the back of his hand, and kissed her. Her lips were cold under his.

"Don't blame you for standin' up for that pa of your'n, old girl. Would do the same in your place. But don't stand in the way of others. And let me do all the managin' there's to be done, myself. Feelin' all right?"

She nodded in the dimness. She leaned against his shoulder, his arm still about her. A pleasant exhaustion overwhelmed her. Then through her fatigue a face formed itself; Ralph's, and her heart contracted with distant pain. She leaned more heavily against John's shoulder; the buggy wheels dipped and swayed in the watery road, on each side stretched the silent fields, shrouded in vapor. There was nothing but silence.

John was restored to good temper. He lifted his hand again and stroked Margaret's cheek.

"Don't worry about it, Mag. I'll talk to Pete alone in the smithy tomorrow. Everythin' will be all right. I'll talk to him tomorrow."

Margaret heard his voice; it was heartening in the pleasurable warmth of her drowsing. She had a sensation that she was drifting away, and she was not afraid. Everything was unimportant.

Chapter Thirteen

But John did not talk to Peter "tomorrow." For, only a few moments before he reached the smithy, Peter Hamilton was dead.

Jim Brownlow had brought his stallion, a huge, black, half-wild animal, to Peter's smithy. The horse was frightened and enraged by this strange man, and reared and struck out with his front legs in an effort to escape him. However, after a few moments Peter's magic with animals partially overcame the beast's fear and he stood quietly, though his flanks quivered and his teeth were bared.

Then Peter made a fatal mistake. He knew animals, but today he was mentally disturbed. Any other time, he would have noticed the danger signals. But he was accustomed to handling difficult animals, and when they finally stood quiet, like this one, he assumed absently that all was well.

He had just bent to take the hoof in his hand when the horse leaped away and struck out with his hind leg. The powerful hoof struck Peter squarely in the forehead, crushing it, toppling him over. Before the horse's startled master could control him, he had struck again and again at the great huddled form on the ground. Then, with a wild, triumphant snort, the horse was off, galloping homeward.

It had all happened in an instant. Jim Brownlow stared blankly from his distantly galloping horse to the bloody mass upon the floor of the smithy. He put out a tentative hand, then recoiled, shuddering.

The April sunlight lay pale and wide upon the earth, in silence. Green shoots were visible over all the basking fields. And then John Hobart rode around the bend, humming to himself. He was astonished to see Jim Brownlow running wildly toward him. He reined in abruptly and waited.

Jim's face was white, ghastly. He pointed back to the smithy and shuddered again. "Pete—" he gasped. "Pete. My horse. Pete. I think he's dead!"

John stared. "Who's—what's dead?" he said roughly. "Stop your shaking, Jim. Who's dead?"

"Pete. Pete Hamilton. It was that stallion of mine—" John dismounted. "Let's go."

With steady, competent hands John examined the mass of bleeding flesh that had been Margaret's father.

"He's dead, all right," he said soberly. He thought of Margaret and frowned. Damn it, what would happen now, and she approaching her eighth month?

They carried Peter home; Pete Hamilton who had loved life. Well, thought John, it's the best way out for him. No sickness, no impatient tossing on a hot bed, no foreknowledge of what was coming.

He was relieved to discover that the widow was so ill today that she could not comprehend what had happened. He sent for Dr. Webster and remained until the physician arrived. It was too late for Peter, but the doctor informed John that Melinda had typhoid fever. The three younger children were also feverish, and were ordered to bed. Linda alone was well. Susan Blodgett was sent for, and she arrived just before John left, full of discriminations.

Looks like the whole lot of 'em's goin', thought John, riding home slowly in the pale wash of spring sunshine. Everythin' seems to happen at once.

He went to see his aunt for the first time in weeks.

She was out in the garden, kneeling in the wet rich earth, and looked up at him in dour silence as he approached. Then she stood up, wiping her hands on her apron.

"What's the matter?" she asked abruptly.

"Pete Hamilton. He was killed by a horse this morning. And Melinda, she's got typhoid fever, and so have all the kids except the oldest. Nice mess. Don't expect Melinda to live to morning. Must be that damn stagnant water they got down there."

Betsy was silent for a few moments. Then, "And you want me to break the news to Margaret, eh?"

Her lack of emotion at the dreadful news affronted him obscurely.

"Well, yes. Cal'cated you could do it better'n me. A woman—"

Without another word she went toward the new house. John remained in the garden. She looked back at him.

"Aren't you coming?"

He flushed uncomfortably. "I'll wait awhile." He walked off toward the barns. At the doorway of one of them he paused and looked over the countryside. The fields ranged from soft yellowish green to dark blue-green, seemingly asleep in the sunset. But he felt their vigor, their passionate life, their eternal promise of harvest. For the first time he was conscious of a hidden sadness. He was not articulate; he had no words to express the dim bulking of his thoughts, though Margaret would have been surprised that he even had such thoughts. He thought of Pete Hamilton.

He wished to put all the subtleties his mind thought into definition, but he could not. He could only be sad, oppressed by the weight of the mighty things he could not sculpture into words.

He had always taken deep and personal satisfaction in the contemplation of his hundreds of acres, the promise of their yield, but today, as he looked at them, he felt humble and small. Somehow, they did not seem to belong to him; he was presumptuous if he thought that. They were merely lent to him, precariously. Tomorrow, they might belong to someone else. That would not change their form nor their richness; the sun would pour down on them just as benignly.

Within an hour he went, afraid, back to his house. Miss Betsy was in the dining room, sharply supervising the setting of the table. John noticed that she had set a third place. He was suddenly enormously relieved. He was afraid of being alone this first night of grief with his wife.

"How's Maggie?" he asked in a low voice. Miss Betsy glanced at him briefly.

"She's got sense," she replied. "I told her right out. She's all right. Lying down a spell. She knows she's got to take care of herself. She's not a complete fool." She laid down a knife. "She's not going down there. Too much danger of getting the fever. She decided that, herself. No, she isn't crying. She started to, then stopped."

When Margaret came down to supper she was very quiet, though deathly pale. She ate barely anything, and seemed confused when she caught John's solicitous gaze. Then, halfway through the meal she said steadily, "I'm glad you've arranged everything, John. Aunt Betsy said you got the doctor, and took care of—things. I'm going to send Mabel over there tomorrow; she's had the fever."

John reddened. "Oh, I didn't do anythin'! Leastways, not more than anyone would do. I'll send over some things in the morning, and go over, myself."

Miss Betsy spoke little, and then of ordinary things, in a dry and commonplace voice. Margaret sat alone with her thoughts. Through the mist of her grief she cried internally for Ralph, who would understand. She could say nothing to that giant of a man opposite her, who never experienced the gripping pangs of agony. What could he know of love, of an anguish that devoured, yet never completely devoured? What could she tell him of her grief for Peter Hamilton, who had loved life, and who was now dead? Nothing. She hated him with a ripping agony. She sat, rigid and white, mechanically putting food to her lips, and mechanically removing it before it entered her mouth.

And opposite her, John thought, she's sufferin'. I can see that. I wish I could say somethin'. But I can't. Pore Maggie. Somehow, I wish we could get together.

Peter Hamilton was burried in the graveyard, among tall waving grass and ragged trees, far from his ancestors. And the next day Melinda Hamilton was carried there and laid beside him. Margaret did not attend the funerals. She was ill in bed.

She did not know that within four days after Melinda's death the three younger children were also carried into the graveyard and buried near their parents. Therefore, she was exhaustedly surprised one day when John led Linda into her bedroom. The girl's face was white and pinched, her eyes swollen. Then Margaret knew. "Please don't say anything," she said. "They're all dead, except me and Linda. I know."

She turned her head slightly and stared out of the window. Her hair was a shadow on her white cheek.

John shifted on his feet. He wanted to kneel down beside her, to say all the words of comfort that surged in him. But her manner repudiated him.

He cleared his throat. "And here's Linda," he said with false cheerfulness. "She's goin' to stay with us. Thought it would be nice for you—after everythin'. She's a right smart girl, Linda." Margaret did not seem to hear. She still stared through the window at the golden haze of the growing fields. "Maggie, ain't you goin' to say anythin' to us?"

She turned her eyes to him slowly. They looked like black hollows in her face. Speak to you? she thought with passionate contempt. Of what? What could I ever say to you? You haven't any human feelings. Only Ralph—I could speak to Ralph.

Tears rushed into her eyes. John saw them, and he was torn apart. He would have gone to her then, but the sternness on her face repulsed him. He went out, leaving Linda alone with her sister.

"Linda," said Margaret, and burst into sobs. Linda stood stiff and unbending in the middle of the room. In the girl's mind was an undying accusation; devoid of reason, she believed that in some way Margaret was responsible for all this. Ma had said over and over, with prophesying venom, "That fine lady will suffer for the way she's treated her folks some day. Yes, she'll suffer. And it'll be too late. Then she'll cry and try to pretend she don't know nothin' 'bout it. Just let her go on, playin' the grand lady, but someday she'll suffer for all this."

"Johnny came this mornin' and said I was to live with

you folks," said Linda surlily. She twisted her thin fingers together and would not look at her sister.

"That's so nice, Linda. And you'll go to school and learn things, and have pretty dresses and good books—"

Linda made a contemptuous sound. "I don't want no school. It's all plumb foolishness. Ma said so. Pa said so."

Margaret frowned. "You don't know what you're talking about!" she said sharply. "What do you want to do, anyway?"

For the first time a little eagerness came into the girl's face. "Mis' King asked me yesterday to come to work for her. Her hired girl's quittin'. She'll give me three dollars a month. I want to go."

Margaret roused herself angrily. "I don't want to hear anything about that, Linda! What would John say? No, you'll go to school and learn something. Don't you want to learn anything?"

"What for?"

"Well, what else would you want?"

Linda looked awkwardly but reverently about the comfort of the big bedroom. "I'd like to live in a place like this, my own place."

Margaret smiled. "That's simple, then. You must go to school, and perhaps, afterward, you could go to school in Whitmore, or even Williamsburg. Then you would meet young men who could give you a nice home."

Linda shot her a glance of cunning. "You didn't go to school in them places, Maggie, and you got a nice home."

Margaret was silent for a moment. Then she began to speak gently, "Linda, this is a very wonderful world. But you can't realize that unless you learn something about it. When you learn other languages, it helps you understand the people who speak those languages, what they think, what they hope to be. When you learn mathematics, you bring the stars closer to you; you bring the world closer to you. If you are ignorant, you will always remain a child. You can't be a woman without knowledge."

Linda made no comment, but stared through the window. "What do you want me to do here?" she asked abruptly, at last, dismissing Margaret's eager words.

Margaret's lips tightened. She was disappointed but not discouraged.

"You might wash yourself a little," she said. "And you might change that dirty dress. Then go downstairs and Mabel will show you how to set the table."

She turned away from the girl, picked up a book from the bedside table and began to read. But when Linda had left the room, her shoulders lifted contemptuously, Margaret gazed blankly before her. She had to talk to someone about this; she wished Miss Betsy would come over. But she did not. Still, she had to talk, and later, when John tiptoed into the room with exaggerated caution, she felt a warm welcome for him.

"Don't whisper, John," she said and smiled. "I'm not an invalid. Sit down, I want to talk to you."

John sat down. "But listen, Mag, I want to say somethin' to you, first. I know how you feel about ole Margot's graves, and the others. So, know what I did today? I sold your land to the railroad, but I made a bargain. They'll run the rails right close to the graves, but not over them! How do you like that?"

The old controversy no longer seemed important to Margaret. She smiled a vague appreciation. She was concerned only with the living.

"Thank you, John. Now, please listen. I talked to Linda today. I tried to interest her in school. It was like talking to a blank wall. And then she actually said that she wanted to hire herself out, doing housework and farm work!"

John considered this for a few moments. Then he began to speak, hesitatingly. "Well, why not, Maggie? Why not let the girl do what she wants to do, eh? I don't hold with this stuff of tryin' to force people to see things the way we do. Maybe you're right; maybe Linda's right. I don't know. But what's right for you may not be right for Linda. You can't set folks' feet on a hill too high for 'em. Seems to me that you can't learn nothin' you ain't got the ability to know. You could fill Linda chock full of learnin' by memory, but she wouldn't understand what she was spoutin'. It wouldn't be of no use to her. It's the things she wants to learn that'll be useful to her. Nothin' else."

"You're trying to say my sister is a fool, and hasn't the brains to learn anything, John Hobart! You don't care a rap about her, that's all!"

"Now, now, Maggie, don't get on your high horse. Jest because you like books and things like that don't mean that Linda ought to. I ain't sayin' I want her to hire herself out workin' for someone else, but you ought to realize that she ain't fit for the high places." He stood up, frowning. "Seems like I'm bein' pretty good 'bout this, Maggie. I'm willin' the girl should stay here and learn somethin', long's it'll make you feel better. I'm willin' to buy her clothes and give her a roof over her head, and good food, and livin' like a civilized young un, even if she's plain ornery. But, I'm not goin' to have rows around here about her goin' to school, and you frettin' over her and tryin' to make a lady of her. Let the girl be. I think I'm bein' pretty good about this."

You mean you don't care and don't understand, thought Margaret bitterly. You'll stand against me with Linda because you don't want to do anything for her, couldn't understand anything fine that I would want to do for her. You like your ignorance and stupidity; this gives you a chance to be proud of them and think they're better than intelligence.

She made up her mind that Linda would go to the district school in the fall, and in the meantime she let the matter rest.

Chapter Fourteen

THREE DAYS BEFORE her child was born, Margaret walked slowly over the nearer fields. The warm June sun lay on the earth, and on the rich young crops. In Miss Betsy's garden stood the intensely blue spears of delphinium; the rose bushes were a blaze of scarlet. Margaret regretted that she had no garden of her own.

Oh! she thought passionately. There must be something beyond common sense and reason! Granny didn't know everything. I betrayed myself into this because of her, when I might have been happy! I shouldn't have listened. Reason isn't everything. There are other things, that you can only see with your mind. Things that I saw, and Ralph saw.

The thought of Ralph was like a blow. If she could only see him once more, ask him for forgiveness, speak to him and know that he understood. If she could only die, if she would die when the child was born!

The gate clicked, and she started. Miss Betsy was coming into her garden. She glanced at Margaret, but said nothing. She began to cut some roses. Margaret walked over to her heavily, forcing a smile.

"I was just looking at your garden. It's so pretty, Aunt Betsy. I wish I had one."

Miss Betsy clipped another rose. "You could have had one," she said coldly. "But you didn't seem to take any interest."

"Well. Everything happened so quickly, Aunt Betsy. All my folks dying."

Miss Betsy said nothing.

Margaret tried again. "You haven't been over to see me, Aunt Betsy, for a long time."

The older woman did not look at her as she said, "Why

should I? We wouldn't have anything to say to each other."

Her words were like a slap in Margaret's face. "Oh, but we would, Aunt Betsy! You are the only one around here who would understand—"

Miss Betsy looked at her with contempt. "Understand! You're always looking for understanding! Why don't you try understanding someone else besides yourself, Margaret Hamilton? Maybe you would learn something."

Stupefied, Margaret watched her as she went on picking her roses. Her face was warm and resentful, and she felt a trifle ashamed without knowing why.

Miss Betsy did not look at her again, but after a moment she went on, "No, we haven't anything to say to each other—yet. But someday, perhaps we will. Someday. But not now."

She turned away with her stiff stride and went toward the gate. Then she said, without turning to Margaret, "Take some flowers, if you want them."

She went into her house through the kitchen door, slamming it behind her. Margaret remained in the garden for a long time. All her pleasure in it had gone. She was sick with her misery, with her abandonment. She pulled a rose to pieces in her shaking fingers. Then she went home.

Three days later her son was born. She endured the agonies and writhings dumbly, hoping each moment to sink into a pit and be lost in it forever. Dr. Webster praised her fortitude; she did not hear him. Throughout the whole travail she thought of nothing but Ralph; he was like a fixed star in cloudy pain.

During most of her labor John was beside her. She scarcely saw him. Her wet hand slipped repeatedly out of his. John thought, somehow, she don't seem to know or care I'm here. Don't seem to see me. Seems like she's shut me out. Why? And he suffered because of this.

The news had traveled. Mesdames Holbrooks, MacKensie, King, and Brownlow sat below in the parlors, whispering, feeling themselves unwelcome. Miss Betsy, managing everything, did nothing to allay their suspicions. She did not speak to them. She spoke in a hard curt voice to the hired girls, and walked about rapidly.

She had taken an amazing liking to Linda. They understood each other, though few words passed between them. She liked the girl's sulky docility; she taught her much. Linda was quick, sure, direct. There's a girl who knows what she wants, and will have it, in spite of her silly sister, Miss Betsy thought.

It was evening before the child was born, a fine and healthy baby. For a while, in his delight, John forgot his wife. The boy, he announced, would be called Richard, after his grandfather. Margaret, sunken into a stupor, did not care. But that night Miss Betsy laid the child on her arm, and she roused. It seemed as though a thread of fire traveled through her exhausted body, and her arms closed convulsively about the child.

When John came in, she was crying. He was touched; he swallowed, but he could not speak.

She was saying to the child, silently, fiercely, I'll protect you, my darling! I'll save you from common sense and reason and reality. They are all lies. Nothing but the things you think are real! Not hard cash, not hard sense.

Dick, the baby, was a sunny-tempered child, sensitive and somewhat frail after his babyhood. John accused Margaret of "pampering" him. Between husband and wife had risen a sullen dark barrier which neither passed. Or, rather, John could not pass it; Margaret would not. The quarrel over the child was heavily overladen with their private and secret quarrel.

Susan Blodgett had received a large sum for her farm from the railroad and had married Silas Rowe, her hired man. They had bought a large and prosperous farm some ten miles away with the money. This was a hard blow to Margaret, who had employed her aunt as an information post about Ralph. Susan had not used the entire sum from the sale of her old farm to buy the new one. She had sent nearly a thousand dollars to Ralph, who was enabled to buy a share in his employer's paper. This raised his prestige, his salary, and his position. Susan had informed Margaret that Lydia Holbrooks had taken a great interest in Ralph.

Six months after the departure of Susan Blodgett, Margaret received a letter from her, with the triumphant announcement that Ralph had married Lydia, and that they had gone to New York. Lydia's father had died recently, and Lydia had inherited his considerable fortune. Ralph had become a partner in a publishing concern in New York.

For some weeks after receiving this news, Margaret walked about in a stunned state, unbelieving. When she finally realized what had happened, it prostrated her. She saw that, unknown to herself all these years, she had kept a small door open through which Ralph might enter at any time. Now the door was slammed eternally in her face. She became ill. Little was thought of this, because she was again pregnant.

Her old zest in life was eclipsed. She was obsessed by one thought: Did Ralph think of her? Had he forgiven her? Had he forgotten her? She thought of Lydia, thought bitterly that she, Margaret, should be at Ralph's side now, living in a hazy, wonderful world of soft conversation, where words counted, not mortgages. She was drowned in her sick and aching fantasies. Only when she took young Dick upon her knee and allowed him to pull her long hair did those eyes begin to glow again with smiling light.

It was a dreary household, enlivened only by John's good-natured bantering of the sulky Linda, the cries and laughter of the baby, and the quarrels of the hired girls. But when Margaret appeared, uneasy silence fell upon everyone.

The railroad had penetrated through the hill that had divided the farms of Susan Blodgett and Peter Hamilton, and was now running through the latter farm. But the graves had been enclosed in a neat and narrow rectangle of white picket fence. No one tended them; the long grass waved over them.

One day, walking heavily because of her new pregnancy, Margaret went there. Only one grave was marked, that one old Margot's, with a white pine board standing upright. She put her hand on the board, tried to raise before her the face of ole Margot. She finally succeeded, dimly. She was amazed at the hatred that rioted through her, sending wild echoes through her held silence. She left, her knees shaking.

A month before her second son, Gregory, was born, she received a small slim packet from Susan Blodgett, with a triumphant note that informed her that this was a book of poems written by Ralph.

For two days Margaret hid it before daring to open it. A sort of fever fell upon her. Then, alone in her room one hot evening, she read the book.

She was too unsophisticated to notice that the book had been published by the house in which he was a partner. The miracle remained that at last he had had his poems published, that he had stepped into fame.

She began to read. An hour passed; another hour. Then she stared fixedly at one page and did not read on.

Her ear, trained to true beauty in Shakespeare, Milton, Dante, soon discerned that here was no splendor. Pale, exquisite poems, yes, but lifeless. Delicate forms that were incomprehensible. Nowhere could she find maturity, the splendor of wise simplicity.

The book slipped from her hand and fell to the floor. She stared through the window. After a moment she rose abruptly, as though wishing to put an end to thoughts that threatened to destroy her life. She went to the window, pushed back the handsome lace curtains, and looked over the stretch of meadow that it revealed. After that sickly poetry the exuberance of the countryside was like a cold wind in her face. Old Margot had once said: "Here is reality. Here is life."

She turned from the window, weeping. To deprive herself of suffering was to deprive herself of her perverse and secret pleasure. She would not have it. Within an hour she had persuaded herself that she alone was to blame because she could find nothing in Ralph's poems. His subtle words, his measured gestures, were too fine for her grossness.

The old enchantment came back. She wrapped it about her like a shawl. Without it, she would be cold and naked. There would be no reason in the life she had led, in the hatred she had nurtured.

Chapter Fifteen

MARGARET HAD FORCED Linda to go to school, but the girl, after one year, had rebelled, and nothing Margaret could do could persuade her to return. John stood with Linda against Margaret. Though the girl hated him as much as she hated Margaret, she had respect for him. Moreover, she was cunning.

Without guessing the reason, she had sensed the estrangement between husband and wife. Soon she was playing up to it. In all her gestures to him, he felt her partisanship and in gratitude, he sided with the girl at every opportunity. Margaret's efforts at discipline, guidance, were scouted by him. Linda was always right; it was Margaret who was the fool. He began to like the girl; he was unusually generous to her. She accepted everything with her smug and pretty smile; it would have amazed him had he guessed how she hated him.

She was nearly eighteen now, and her blonde loveliness seemed to outshine Margaret's darker beauty. She was tall and slender, soft roses and gold. She dressed with conscious effect; she planned her gestures.

Despite all this, she had few admirers among the eligible young men in the county. She suspected that it was because of Margaret, though she did not know why. But she saw that Margaret did not encourage visitors, that she had no friends. She told herself that it was "because folks see into her."

Ezra King and his wife had two daughters and a son. Parsimonious as they were, they were reluctant to employ a hired girl, and so the daughters did all the house and farm work. Quiet, drab girls, one was never conscious of them in a room. But the son, young Bill, was handsome, arrogant, lazy, the pride of his mother. He had been educated, according to the standard of the country, and gave copious advice about new agricultural methods. Ezra King, after reluctantly testing them, was forced to admit their value, and he developed a profound admiration for his son.

The farm was prosperous though small. John held a heavy mortgage upon it. It might have been paid off, but young Bill liked to travel about the county and to Williamsburg during the winter; he also had his own smart buggy and horse. John had great contempt for the youth, but he seemed pleased when Bill, having noticed Linda for the first time at a church supper, called her. Linda was overwhelmed. She went riding with Bill, and soon it was accepted in the county that she was his girl. Mrs. King at first objected to his courting the sister of Maggie Hamilton, but when John hinted that he might do something for the young couple her objections were silenced. Eventually, she began to make much of Linda.

One day John said to young Bill, half sourly, half good-naturedly, "When you and Linda get hitched, and your dad don't pay me the mortgage, maybe I'll give you both his farm for a weddin' present."

Young Bill merely laughed evasively. He had no intention of marrying Linda.

Little Dick, at four, was pretty, but rather small for his age, and sensitive. He was afraid of his father and deathly afraid of the farm animals, so when John tried to seat him on a horse Dick had violent hysterics. He loved his mother, and fled to her for protection when he heard John's step.

Little Gregory was different. He had his mother's straight black hair and his father's blue eyes. He was a strong, exuberant baby, who screamed with delight when his father tossed him in the air. He adored John; he was restive with Margaret. When he was two, and Dick five, he had already developed a feeling of superiority over his shy and gentle brother. Dick would sit quietly near his mother; Gregory's sturdy legs usually scampered over the yard and the garden.

Margaret loved both her children, but from the first she had felt alien to Gregory. There was something about Dick which reminded her painfully of Ralph. Because of this she protected him. He would have his chance.

She had heard, through Susan Blodgett, that Ralph had a child, a pretty little girl, and that he and his wife were doing well in New York. "He's got a twelve-room house, now," wrote Susan proudly. "And three hired girls." She wrote to Margaret only when she wished to convey news of Ralph's increasing success.

Ralph with a wife and child! Margaret still remembered that night so long ago on the hilltop when she had given him what he wanted, out of love and pity. But she didn't remember how she had failed to respond to him, how she had shrunk from that contact. And she didn't compare this with the still violent upsurge of her blood when John held her to him. When he took her, she forgot everything, even that she loved Ralph.

For the rest of the time she had made him miserable with her silences, her remotenesses, her pale face. And quarreled with him at every occasion.

Chapter Sixteen

Bɪʟʟ Kɪɴɢ ʜᴀᴅ ʙᴇᴇɴ ᴄᴏᴜʀᴛɪɴɢ Linda for two years, and they were no nearer marriage. Then, quite suddenly, he dropped her.

Linda's face became pinched, dazed and absent. She avoided John, where she had sought him out before.

One day Margaret had gone for a drive with the children and returned earlier than expected. She entered the cool dimness of the house, and found Linda crouched on the lower steps of the staircase, weeping bitterly. She had bent her head upon her knees in an attitude of abandoned despair. Margaret sat down beside her, put her arm over the thin shoulders.

"Linda," she said urgently. "Won't you tell me about it, dear?"

Linda lifted her head, but she flung Margaret's arm away with viciousness. She tried to get up, but Margaret tightened her hands suddenly on the girl's shoulders.

"Linda, you've got to tell me. I want to help you."

Linda laughed shortly. "*You* help me!" she cried. "You don't want to help me! Look what you did to pore Ma!"

Margaret had heard this accusation a dozen times before, but her depression had made her indifferent. Now, she faced it squarely.

"Just what did I do to Ma, Linda? Come on, I've heard this before, but now I want it brought out. What did I do?"

And Linda could say nothing. Just what had Maggie done? Linda had never really said, though she had accused Maggie obscurely.

"You ought to know!" she burst out at length. "Ma knew, and you knew! She didn't tell me just what." A fury rose up in her against Margaret, and she struggled

128

to her feet. Margaret stood up, too; her face was pale and grim.

"Linda, there was nothing, except that Ma always hated me ever since I can remember."

"I don't believe you!" spat the girl. "Ma always said you'd suffer some day for what you did to her, so there must have been somethin'. And, I 'spect you are sufferin', with the way you drag yourself around, and I'm glad of it! I'd like to see you die! You ain't even good to John, even though he gives you everythin' and don't expect you to work like other wimin. Everyone talks how you treat him like dirt, and laughs behind your back!"

For a moment Margaret stared at her, her face expressionless. Then she struck Linda heavily across the cheek. The girl staggered back, caught hold of the newel post to save herself from falling, and cried out when she saw Margaret advancing again upon her. She flung up her arm to defend herself.

Margaret, from the excess of her rage and obscure shame, would have struck again and again, but, despite the dimness of the hall, she saw something in the girl's figure. She halted abruptly. Linda was sniffling abjectly, her face in the crook of her elbow. Margaret seized her wrists in one powerful hand, grasped the back of the girl's hair, and made her face her.

"So that's the trouble!" she said in a low voice. "You—you. Who was it—Bill King? Bill King? Answer me, you dirty little cat!"

Linda struggled in Margaret's grasp, twisting from side to side. She began to sob; but she could not free herself.

"I won't tell you!" she cried thickly. "Don't hit me, Maggie! I'll tell you! Yes, it was Bill! And now he won't marry me! He promised to marry me!"

Margaret released her so suddenly that she fell backwards again, and again caught hold of the newel post. She stared at her sister in terror. But Margaret's rage had only been assumed to force the truth from the girl. Actually, she was filled with compassion and protective love.

"Hush, Linda! Stop making all that noise. Do you want

Mary and Mabel to hear you, way out in the kitchen? Come into the parlor. I want to talk to you."

With the door shut, Margaret began, "Let's talk about this sensibly, Linda. Where's Bill now? I haven't seen him for three months."

Linda sobbed chokingly. "He—he's gone away. To Williamsburg. He must'a told his Pa and Ma. When I went over there the other day, Miz' King shut the door in my face and hollered through it, 'Go 'way! You ain't goin' to find out nothin' 'bout my boy, you bad girl.'"

Margaret's eyes flashed ominously, but she only said quietly, "Go on, Linda."

"I went to Ezra, too. I said, 'Mist' King, Bill's got to marry me. You got to tell me where he is. Maybe he don't know about me.' And he said, kind of gloatin', 'Yes, he does, but he ain't gonna be forced to marry a gal like you. He ain't gonna be a father to someone else's young un.' And he walked away and shouted to the cows so that he wouldn't hear me no more."

Margaret's face was sick. "And so the whole county knows about it now! God!"

"I don't want you to do nothin', Maggie. I—I love Bill. If he don't want to marry me, it's all right. I—I'll go away. I'll go somewheres. I don't mind nothin' any more."

She fell into a chair and covered her face with her hands. Margaret looked at her with bitter pity. Somewhere she had failed. No, it was Melinda who was the cause of this. Her hatred had poisoned anything that might have been between Linda and herself; Linda was a victim of that hatred.

She touched the girl's head gently.

Linda did not appear for supper, and John and Margaret sat down alone. They barely spoke to each other these days; the meal usually passed in silence. Margaret watched him. He kept his head down and ate stolidly; a few gray hairs had appeared in the blackness of his hair; beneath it his skin was burned a deep red-brown and was rough with faint webbing.

Linda's words suddenly repeated themselves in her, and she felt a pang of remorse. She had treated him badly;

she might have forgotten herself a little, for his sake. It was not his fault that she loved Ralph; she had been unjust to him.

"John," she said quietly. "John, I want to talk to you."

He glanced up warily. "What is it?"

He hates me too, she thought sadly. It's my fault. I never speak to him unless I want something. "John," she said. "I want to talk about Linda."

He made an abrupt gesture of dismissal. "I ain't goin' to talk about Linda! Got more important things on my mind. Not that they'd interest you, though," he added shortly.

She felt, under his words, his resentment and deep hurt. She opened her mouth to speak, then stopped; words would never set things right between them. It was too late for that.

But John was really pleased that Margaret wanted to talk to him, if it were only about Linda. After a moment, he said, "Saw Ezra King today. Asked me for an extension, and I said, 'Why not?' So, we're goin' to the bank tomorrow to sign up again."

"John! I want to talk to you about the Kings!" So, he had not heard yet. "And, it's about Linda, too. You know Bill was courting her, and now he's gone away."

John shrugged. "If she can't keep a man, what you want me to do? She's got to work that kind of thing out for herself."

Margaret kept down her anger. "But," she said slowly and steadily, "I've got to mind her business now, John. You see, Linda's in trouble; Bill got her in trouble."

He dropped his fork and stared at her, his mouth open. "Eh? What's this you're sayin'? Linda in trouble? Bill? What the hell is this? Think I'm goin' to have my house disgraced by such goin's on? Well, she can pack her bag and get out of here. I'll not have it, y'hear?"

"That's just the point, John. She can't go to him. He promised to marry her, but his father sent him away."

He fell silent, scowling. She tried to follow his thoughts; she watched the dark blood coming into his face. Then he deliberately picked up his fork again and ate. She clenched her fists tightly, and waited. He swallowed his coffee. Then he put down the cup and regarded her with something vicious in his face.

"Can't blame them, in a way. What do you ever do to try to be neighborly to 'em? 'Spect this is their way of gittin' back at you. Not good enough for you, eh? Well, they're showin' you now that your sister ain't good enough for 'em. Linda'll get out of this the best way she can. And she can't stay in my house after tomorrow, no, ma'am!'"

He's trying to hurt me, to repay me, she thought bitterly. He's never had the upper hand before. Well, I can't blame him, much. I'm ashamed to plead with him, when I ignore him other times. She stood up.

"All right, then, John. I'll go to see them, myself. Linda's my sister. And she can't leave here, until she leaves right. If she goes, I'll have to go with her."

He smiled sourly. "Fine talkin'. But it don't mean a thing, Maggie. Sounds high and mighty like a book, but this is real life. Where'd you both go? Bah!"

In spite of herself, she began to cry weakly. He looked at her for a long time, and his face became somber. He turned his coffee cup several times in its saucer. *She ought to know I don't mean that,* he thought. *I couldn't let Maggie go, not for a minute! If she'd only give me a chance. I can't make her out, noways. She used to be so gay, so strong and full of life. Now, she drags around, looking sick, and someway lettin' me know it's all my fault. She don't know it, but she loves me. Somethin' stops her from knowin' that. Wish't there was some way of lettin' her know it.*

He put out his hand. "Sit down, Maggie," he said gently. " 'Spect we can talk this out sensible, 'thout gettin' all stirred up about it. You know I like Linda. She's got sense. No use you gettin' bothered. Got to think of your own young uns, and the other one that's comin' soon. Hell, I'm sorry I said those things to you 'bout Linda. I want to help her, sure. But, you ain't never tried to be friendly with folks. Even ole Miz' Holbrooks don't come avisitin' no more. I ain't sayin' I want a house full of gossipin' wimin-folks, but nobody don't come 'cept the men on business. Folks're scared to death of us. They don't mind me, but they sure hate you, Maggie. I'm not sayin' you ought to care about that, but with a gal like Linda in the house, and our young uns growin' up, things ought to be different. You might've made friends in the county, but you didn't. Now most of 'em would cut your throat in a minit. Hate to think of leavin' you a widow!" He chuckled.

"Now then, I'll go to Ezra King, tomorrow, and I'll say, 'If your boy don't marry Linda Hamilton right away, you kin just pack up your parcels and leave. The farm's mine. And I'll give it to some young feller that'll marry her. So smoke that a while."

Margaret's pale face glowed with gratitude. "John! I—I can't thank you for this. Linda will, but somehow, I can't say anything. I should have known you wouldn't turn your back on me—"

He got up and kissed her. She pressed her head against his arm, and as usual the flow of his strength comforted her; her tears wet his sleeve. In a little while she ran upstairs, calling happily. But the girl's room was empty. Margaret returned to the parlor where John was just lighting a lamp and humming through the pipe gripped in his teeth.

"John," she said anxiously. "Linda isn't here. Where could she have gone?"

"She can't've gone far," replied John. "Maybe she's upstairs with the kids. Don't she usually sing the baby to sleep?"

Nevertheless, he went upstairs with Margaret. Despite her pregnancy, she moved with the hurried step of anxiety. The nursery was dim and silent. The two little boys lay in their flounced beds, asleep. The white curtains blew and a star shone in one window. The room was filled with the peace and evening fragrance of the quiet countryside beyond the house. Momentarily forgetting Linda, Margaret tiptoed to the small beds, bent over them. Even in the darkness of the room John could see the warm indulgent smile she bestowed on little Gregory, as though she felt some secret amusement. But she bent over little Dick with a sudden movement, as though of protection, and she did not smile. She kissed his forehead, slowly, and smoothed his fine dark hair.

John watched her. For a moment, in the twilight, he saw the woman Margaret had been, the woman who might be. It was as though these two forms stood on each side of the real Margaret, who was pale, subdued, depressed. He felt a great sadness; somewhere the real woman had been lost, this was a strange and alien creature. No one lost her, he thought. She's lost herself.

She was still engrossed with Dick, straightening the quilts on his bed; so it was that only John heard a far and startled shout, the sound of running feet. He went to the window. Jack Winslow, his foreman, and three of the farm hands appeared at the barn door and stared at the new house through the dusk. John leaned through the window, called to them. Jack began to speak but stopped abruptly. Margaret's pale face had appeared at his shoulder and Jack had seen it. His wildly gesturing hands fell to his side. He began to speak again, and John could hear the strain of his voice.

"Hey, John, better come out to the barn. Ole red-eye's broke his leg, or somethin'."

Instantly John knew that he lied. He turned to his wife.

"Say, Mag, my prize bull's hurt himself. Wait downstairs for me a minit, will you? And then we'll get Linda and talk this thing over, all of us."

Margaret nodded indifferently. She was never interested in any of the farm matters. She heard John running through the hall downstairs and out the door. But she heard the sounds with only her external ear; she was listening to the breathing of the children.

Suddenly it seemed to her that that breathing was infinitely sad. The children would not always sleep so; there were nights of pain and despair ahead for them, and in those nights she could do nothing. It would have been better if they had never been born.

She moved stiffly to the door. There was a dry and sickening sensation in her throat. Her hands were cold and numb as she started down the stairs. The front door opened, and John and Miss Betsy came into the hall, and stared up at her in the light of the swinging lamp.

Margaret stopped dead and clutched the banister with a slipping hand.

"Linda," she said hoarsely.

John started up the stairs toward her; he held out his hands.

"Linda—she got hurt, bad hurt," he said. "Look, Maggie, you've got to lie down a while. Aunt Betsy'll stay with you while I go see—what can be done for Linda." He was sweating desperately; Margaret's face, upturned to his, had turned gray. He could not tell her what they had found in the barn—Linda hanging from the rafters, quite dead. But she seemed to read it in his trembling flesh, his wet hands. She still stared at him blindly as he released her to Miss Betsy in the bedroom, continued to stare at him as the older woman laid her on the bed. He cursed Linda wildly to himself; to do this to Maggie, who was going to have a baby in three months. If the poor girl would only say something to show that she knew nothing.

But Margaret knew that Linda was dead, that she had killed herself. For hours she was very quiet. Then her physical agony began.

She almost died before dawn. She had lost the baby, a little girl. John, who had been able to control himself up to now, broke down entirely at the sight of his dead daughter. Somehow, even Margaret's journey to the edge of death did not affect him so; it was as if he had lost something ineffably precious.

It was not for several days, long after Linda had been hurriedly buried, that the doctor could say that Margaret might recover. John could come and go, knowing he was recognized, that Margaret had actually smiled at him as she lay sunken in her pillows. She had wasted terribly; there were black shadows beneath her dull eyes.

She did not speak of Linda, nor of the baby she had lost. She seemed to have forgotten them both.

Chapter Seventeen

BUT MARGARET HAD NOT FORGOTTEN. During the long slow weeks that followed, she had been busy remembering. And planning. What she had planned restored her strength more quickly than did her powerful constitution.

During her recovery she had many visitors; she received them all amiably, thanked them for jellies and broths and cakes. But she never ate any of them. She would eat nothing made by the hands of those she thought had murdered Linda. However, whenever Mrs. King called, smiling uneasily, Margaret received her kindly. She had lots of time.

Her aunt, Mrs. Susan Rowe, drove ten miles to visit her, and remained a week. Susan had become plump, complacent and overbearing. She still had rancor against her niece, and showed it openly even while sitting beside Margaret's bed.

One day she said, "Maggie, did I tell you Ralph and dear Lydia was visitin' me last spring?"

"No, you didn't tell me." Margaret's voice was quiet. She was sitting up with the aid of pillows, her black hair braided on each side of her thin face. She was knitting and her hands did not slow.

"Well, they was. You wouldn't know Ralph. He got real fat. And Lydia, too. They've got another little girl, now, makin' two. Phyllis is only three, and they've named the baby after me—Susan. Ain't that nice? They got four servants and a hired girl for the babies and two carriages, one to take Ralph where he wants to go, and one for Lydia and the young uns! They was there when it was my birthday, and Ralph, bless him, gave me two hundred dollars! They're real happy, and Lydia thinks the sun rises and sets on my boy."

She chattered on, her sly eye upon Margaret. Margaret was tranquil. But she thought, so you were here, Ralph, and you never came to see me. You were only ten miles away! And you never came. You must have known what I have been suffering. Just as I know what you have been suffering. Only you and I could have told each other about it.

Then all at once it seemed as though she could not endure it, as though living had become unbearable. She had to see Ralph; she had to see him. It did not matter what they tore down, what they trod on to reach each other.

When she could speak, she said casually to Susan: "I want to know Ralph's address. I want to write to him and tell him how much I enjoyed his book."

Susan hesitated, then with ill grace she gave Margaret Ralph's address.

Resolved now, to write to Ralph and beg him to see her when he came again, Margaret's physical slackness vanished. She sat up alertly when Miss Betsy brought the children in to see her, she was delighted, kissed them, fondled them. She scolded Gregory when he teased his older brother, gathered Dickie to her breast and looked coldly at the other child. Miss Betsy watched her. When John came in, smelling of clean hay and cattle, she greeted him pleasantly, almost gaily. As she talked to him, she thought, I'm done with you. She said to him, "Yes, I'm much better, John. I think I can get up for a while tomorrow."

John watched her, pleased but uneasy. There seemed something false in her animation, in her desire to conciliate him. It appeared to him that there was something mocking beneath her words. Though she laughed at his heavy humor, let him hold her hand, he felt that she was farther from him than ever, that she had at last closed a door between them.

Driven by uneasiness, he went for a long walk over his land in the late summer twilight. He walked rapidly and unevenly, smelling the pungency of sun-warmed hay, the incense of coming autumn.

Gradually, he felt strangely comforted. It seemed to him that while a man walked so, on his own land, among his own harvests, that nothing of great harm could come to him.

When he returned to the house he felt courageous again, and he felt a great pity for Margaret, so removed these days from the strength of the earth. It made him sad that she had once known its power and that she did not know it now. Why, that was why he had loved her in the first place, because she loved the things he loved, because she too was unshakable and strong. But now, she looked at nothing, saw nothing, but some sickness in herself. What that sickness was he did not know clearly, but he knew it was there.

He had a shamefaced impulse to pray. He had not prayed for a long time, since he was a child. But he awkwardly removed his hat, lifted his face to the evening sky, and tried. He could not form words; he could only think in confused shapes, in great yearning gestures. And somehow he felt that he had been understood.

He would not have felt so comforted had he known that Margaret was, at that very minute, writing a long and incoherent letter to Ralph Blodgett.

Margaret sat at her bedroom window, wrapped in shawls. The early autumn air was chilly, but the sun shone with brilliance. Her hands lay on her knees slackly.

I have nothing, now, except Dickie and Ralph, she thought. I feel as though I had been in a dream for a long time, and heard voices only at a distance. Now everything is painfully bright; it has a meaning. Oh, it's glorious to be alive again, tingling. I have only to wait now, until Ralph comes to me.

Miss Betsy brought little Gregory in to see her. Margaret kissed the child absently, then pushed him away. "Take him out," she said irritably. "He tires me. He's so noisy. When Dickie comes in, I want to see him."

She did not see the look of hurt on the child's face. He had not understood her words, but he had felt her repudiation. He went to Miss Betsy and hid his face in her skirts. She put her hand on his head.

"You don't treat this poor baby right, Maggie," she said quietly.

"Oh, don't be sentimental, Aunt Betsy. He's just a little animal. He's not got any feelings to be hurt." No more than his father has, she added to herself.

Miss Betsy felt a harsh constriction in her throat. "How do you know he hasn't any feelings?" she burst out, "Just because he hasn't silly feelings like yours doesn't mean he hasn't his own kind! You don't deserve to have him, that you don't!"

She gathered the child in her arms and strode from the room. Margaret felt somewhat ashamed. But she shrugged, and resumed her contemplation of the country beyond the window. She did not look at it with friendliness; it belonged to John. She had no part in it, never wanted any part in it. Now, she was done with it forever. She saw no more beauty in the hills and the valleys and the changing sky.

The bedroom door opened silently; Mrs. Ezra King, clad in gray calico, gray sunbonnet and gray shawl, stood in the doorway. Margaret looked at her without expression; she knew why the woman had come.

Mrs. King advanced into the room, after glancing nervously behind her. The house was silent.

"Maggie, I 'spect you know why I come?"

Margaret said nothing. She did not offer the visitor a chair. She merely looked at her steadfastly. Mrs. King put a handkerchief to her mouth, her hand was trembling.

"You kin help us, Maggie, if you want to. And I know you will. I said to Ezra this mornin', 'Maggie will help us. Maybe she don't know about it. Johnny Hobart'll listen to her.' "

"Yes, he'll listen," said Margaret quietly. "But you see, I won't speak to him." She looked at the woman with hatred. "You killed Linda, you know, Sarah King."

Mrs. King's face went gray. Her mouth moved without sound. Then she put her recticule on the table and faced Margaret with a spare dignity.

"Now, you know that ain't so, Maggie Hamilton. If your sister had behaved herself, like a decent girl, maybe Bill might've married her. 'Sides, if you only knew what that girl used to say 'bout you to all of us, when she'd come over and visit with me! Many times I said, 'Lindy Hamilton, you ought to be 'shamed, and Maggie so good to you!' But she didn't have no shame, Maggie. The girl's dead, and I hope she's in peace, but she was a bad girl in more ways than one, and even before her trouble I didn't want Bill to have no truck with her. This is plain speakin', Maggie Hamilton, and I wouldn't've said nothin' 'bout it, but you made me. Only you was allus one never to see things as they are."

Margaret's face darkened, became ugly with passion. But she said quietly, "However, it still remains that you killed Linda. She was only a young girl, almost a child. You had no pity for her. So, I have no pity for you."

Mrs. King drew herself up.

"It ain't only Linda, Maggie Hamilton. That ain't the only reason you're drivin' us out of house and home, out of the place that Ezra's pa owned, and his pa's pa before him! That ain't the reason we're put on the road, and maybe on the county! You allus hated me—all of us. You hate the whole country! I've allus seen that. I said to Miz Holbrooks, 'Maggie's dangerous. She hates all of us. It's a bad thing for us that she married Johnny Hobart!'"

Margaret stood up, grasping the back of her chair. "You're right!" said Margaret exultantly. "I hate you; I hate all of you! I remember things, you see. I hate your ugliness and your stupidity, your meanness and your greed. I'll not be satisfied until I turn all of you out, and I'll do it! Now then, get out of here!"

She sat down again; she was almost gasping. But Mrs. King had become calm. She looked at Margaret steadily.

"So you've come right out and spoke your piece, Maggie Hamilton. You hate us. I 'spect it's because we've allus hated you. No, not hated you, but laughed at you, and your whole family. And then when you married Johnny Hobart, we was ready to be friends with you, because you'd become decent and like civilized folks. But you wouldn't be friends. You had no sense. How could we like you 'fore you got married? What was there 'bout you to like? We thought you'd change when you got married. Well, you changed, sure enough. But how? You became mean and haughty, looked down on us like we was dirt, not answerin' us when we met you on the road. And now I believe what Linda said 'bout you: that you treat your man like he was dirt, too, not good enough to touch your little finger.

"You got a lot to learn, Maggie Hamilton. And you'll learn, true's there's a Lord in heaven! And all I hope is that you'll suffer like you made us suffer, drivin' us off our land, makin' beggars of us. You'll have the whole county against you and your man. There won't be no peace for you. Johnny Hobart's a hard man, but he was good in his way, givin' decent folks time. Now you'll turn the whole county against him, too, and there won't be peace for him either."

"Get out, with your pious whinings," said Margaret contemptuously. "Or shall I have put you out?"

When John came in for the noonday meal Margaret called him. He came running up the stairs two at a time, eagerly. He found her pale and smiling. She told him about Mrs. King. He listened, his face becoming heavy.

Then he said, "See here, Maggie. I'm puttin' them out because I need their land, and they're three years behind to me. Ezra King's no farmer. His land's goin' to rack and ruin. He ain't shiftless, just not fitten to be a farmer. I'm apayin' him five hundred dollars, though I don't need to.

"Now then, I might've let them stay, 'spite of Linda. Linda was your business. The girl was soft inside. It wasn't no quarrel of mine. But another reason I'm makin' them go is because of the baby that—died. I can't forget that baby."

Margaret smiled indulgently, began to speak of something else. But when he left her, he was vaguely disturbed. He had noticed lately that though his neighbors still treated him with respect, they whispered together in groups after he had passed. He looked down on them, but, paradoxically, wanted their regard. He had a jovial nature that desired a sympathetic audience. But now, when he met his neighbors in the general store and joked as usual with them, they merely stared at him without comment.

Chapter Eighteen

THE FIRST PART OF AUTUMN was as dry as summer. The long drought continued until well into October. Then, about the fifteenth, the heavens opened.

After three days, when the falling wall of water did not show any signs of thinning, the river began to rise. It rose within a foot or two of its banks, a phenomenon never seen in that generation. The country folk became uneasy; they stood in thick groups about the river, watching the muddy and rushing waters with deep gloom. If it kept on, there would be a flood. The late crops were already being destroyed; down the valley there were reports of lost cattle, where the river had risen higher.

And still it rained, and still the river rose. There were reports from distant places that houses were being swept from their foundations. All the bridges had become unsafe; only the one at Big Bend, between the valley and Whitmore, was showing no signs of weakness. And then, after two weeks, all the bridges but that one went down, the lower valley was flooded, scores of cattle were lost, and there were several deaths reported in isolated parts of the valley.

Even when the rain stopped the streams continued to rise, swollen, red-brown, ferocious; trees sent bridges thundering down, swept whole herds to death, and spread a watery desolation over two-thirds of the valley. Each day brought reports of other deaths, of children and old people, and even of strong men and young women.

John Hobart suffered the least. His lower acres were inundated, but two-thirds of his land was still above water, and there had been no threat to his home. The house was situated on rising land; though from the windows, to the east, could be seen shining breadths of water where green fields had been. At night they could hear the distant thundering of the river, but they knew they were safe.

The Hobarts, the Brownlows, the Kings, the Holbrooks, and the MacKensies escaped most of the general destruction, as did another half-dozen families. But for the rest, there was only bereavement and ruin.

Everyone lent his hand, his home, and his fires to aid the sufferers. Personal differences went down before common sympathy as the land and the bridges had gone down before the flood. But for a few days John Hobart did nothing.

Then one night he came to Margaret, who was sewing before the fire as her two little boys played on the hearth. He came in, muddy and tired, his boots squishing water on the clean rugs. Gregory rose up with a shout at the sight of his father, struggled on his short legs to him, his hands outstretched. But Dickie merely glanced up idly, then leaned against his mother's knee. She laid a gentle hand on his head, and they smiled at each other.

John's tired face lit with a fond smile as Gregory clung to his great legs, then he swung the child up in his arms. Gregory sat on his shoulder, and, carrying the child so, John approached his wife.

"Maggie," he said abruptly. "Aunt Betsy's movin' in here tonight. I'm turnin' the old house over to the folks that need it. 'Bout three, four families. They ain't got no place to go, and everybody else's crowded. So, you'd better get out any blankets you can spare, and vittles and coal oil, and look down in the cellar and see what you got that can go over there. Jack and I and the other fellows'll carry them over right away. The folk'll be here in a minit or two; a whole hay wagon full of 'em."

Margaret continued to sew for a few moments; then she put her work on the table beside her and rose. She looked directly into John's eyes; her lips had whitened.

"I have nothing to give these—people, John," she said calmly. "Nothing."

He stared at her as though he had not heard right. Then dark color rushed into his face, and he sputtered, "What's that? What's that you say, Maggie? You ain't got nothin'? That's a lie. We've got enough for fifty people, a hundred people. We've got—"

"We've got—nothing," said Margaret. Her voice was very quiet, but she was ashen. "I've got nothing for them. Not a crust of bread, not a blanket. I won't have them here. I won't lift my hand for them. You can do what you want with them, keep them, turn them out to starve or rot. I'll have nothing to do with them."

In spite of her quietness there was something so violent in her manner that John turned cold. He let Gregory slip out of his arms; he took Margaret's arm in his strong fingers, held her close to him.

"Do you know what you're sayin'? Before God, I don't believe it! Turn those folks away? Not give them somethin' to eat? Not put a roof over 'em? Folks that've lost every damn thing in the world? Everybody's taken in all they can. They can't take no more. Do you understand that, Maggie? Are you sick—in the head?"

She pulled her arm from him, sprang back a step and faced him. All the accumulated hatred of the years rushed out upon her face.

"You fool!" she cried. "How could I expect you to understand? Don't you know I've waited all my life for just this minute? I've hoped for a chance to do just this, to have them coming begging at my door, and then to turn them away. I've watched them watching me, hoping in their black hearts that something would happen to me, something that would leave me at their mercy. But now they're at my mercy. And I'm going to show them none."

John seemed more aghast at her manner and her words than he did at their meaning. Was this Maggie, this half-wild creature with bloodless lips and glaring eyes? He was terrified. He took her by the shoulders, shook her a little.

"Maggie, you ain't well," he said hoarsely. "Maggie, darling, sit down. There now, sit down just a minit, and listen to me. What's wrong with you? Somethin' botherin' you? Got that pain in your head again? Maggie, look at me. Honey, stop that shiverin' and look at me. Look, Maggie, want me to send for ole Dr. Brewster? I'll send the trap for him—"

She shook off his hands. She pushed her hair from her forehead. She shook her head jerkily.

"Oh, what's the use, anyway?" she sobbed dryly. "Leave me alone, John. You couldn't understand. You always were stupid. You never understood, nor cared, what I thought about you. You never cared to know how I've hated you all this time, dreaded the sight of you, wanted to run from you. You've done only what you wanted to do; you never cared to ask what I wanted to do. And now, when you've got a chance to help me you ask me if I'm sick! Yes, I am—sick. Sick of you, sick of all these people, sick of everything. I only want to get away from you."

John stood before the fire, staring at Margaret, his hands hanging slack at his sides. His eyes were empty, his face the color of wet clay. The little boys began to whimper. A long silence fell, broken only by the sound of the dropping coals and the distant creak of a heavily loaded cart. Margaret did not look at her husband; her head had fallen back against the chair; her eyes were closed. But in the firelight he could see the throb of the pulse in her white throat. She looked exhausted and infinitely broken.

John felt as if his whole world had fallen about him with an enormous crash. He turned from his wife; he was swallowing hard. He put a hand on the mantelpiece, supported himself by it. He seemed to sag.

"They're here, John," said Miss Betsy from the doorway. "I've sent the girls to look for things, and you'd better call the men and have them taken over to the house."

Very slowly John turned to her. His aunt stood in the doorway, a black shawl about her head and shoulders, the wool glistening with drops of water. Though her controlled expression did not change, her eyes were bitter with compassion. How long she had been there, how much she had heard, neither husband nor wife knew. The children stood on the hearth, side by side, staring.

"All right, Aunt Betsy," said John heavily. He looked for a moment at Margaret; she did not stir. "All right," he repeated. His step, as he went toward his aunt, was slow and heavy, as though he had suddenly become old. When he had gone, Miss Betsy stood there and looked at Margaret. Then she too slowly went out.

After a long while Margaret sat upright. She began to sob. The tears rushed over her cheeks. She struck her hands together. She sobbed for several minutes without control. Something ached in her chest and she did not understand it.

John worked for hours among the families in the old house and Miss Betsy worked with him. Lights glowed from every window; a lamp was set in the attic where three men and six boys were bedded. Margaret was left alone in the deserted house with the two children; she put them to bed. Little Gregory fell asleep immediately, his fist in his cheek, but Margaret knelt beside Dickie's bed and held his hand. The child watched her gravely in the dim light. She held his hand suddenly against her breast.

"Oh, Dickie, Dickie!" she whispered. "If I could only talk to you! Dickie, I'll take you away from here!"

"Yes, Mamma," said Dickie, uncomprehending.

"I'm going to protect you!" she whispered fiercely. And then it seemed to her that a cold and detached voice asked: "From what?" She stood up, puzzled. From what? She could see the lights of the old house through the window, could see the passing shadows of those who were making the refugees comfortable. She pulled the shutters closed against the night and went from the room.

Downstairs she sat before the fire. She tried to sew, to read, but could not. The clock chimed nine, then ten. John had not returned. She went up to her room. The hearth was gray with ashes. She built a fire, shivering in the dank chill, and then sat before it.

She had fallen asleep in her chair when she heard the door open and John come in. She did not turn to him, though the painful throbbing had begun in her chest again. She knew that he stood for a long time, watching her. Then he went to his chest of drawers and began to pull blankets from it.

"Those are the only ones left, John," she said sharply. He continued to pull bedding from the drawer for several moments before he answered. He did not look at her.

"I want them for myself," he said expressionlessly. "I'm movin' over to the bedroom across the hall."

She stood up; her right temple began to pound and she put up her hand to stop it.

"You mean—you're going to sleep over there tonight?"

"Yes. And every night."

She stared at him. He looked exhausted and dirty. She took a step toward him, then stopped. She pressed her hands together and swallowed.

"It's cold and unaired over there, John. We haven't used it since Greg was born. Wait, I'll get sheets for you, and some fresh pillows—"

"I don't want you to do nothin' for me—ever," he said. He clutched the blankets in his arms and started toward the door on stumbling feet.

"John!" she cried. "Wait, just a minute. John, I'm—sorry for what I said to you tonight! I—I didn't really mean it. Please believe me. I was—just that I hate them so that I wanted to hurt you as you were hurting me, helping them. Please try to understand!"

He stood with his back to her for a long moment; she did not know that she was crying desperately, but it seemed to her that she must stop him at all costs, that if he went out of the room something would be lost to her for all time. When he dropped the blankets on the floor and turned slowly to her, her relief was so great that she sobbed loudly. But his face was still heavy and drained.

"I don't understand you, Maggie." His voice was emotionless. "It wasn't long ago, before Dickie was born, when you wanted me to let young Townsend have more time on account of his six kids. Remember that? You was always doin' somethin' for the no-accounts in Pine Hollow. And then, when I bring these folks to the old house, you raise a row.

"Now, wait a minit. I'm agoin' to do the talkin' for a few minits. I've got a lot to say to you, Mag, and might's well say it now and have it over. I've wanted to for a long time, and I'm agoin' to say them now.

"You hate all the folks hereabouts. You got your reasons. I ain't in love with 'em, either. But that don't mean I can't be friends with 'em. I can't go all my life with everybody against me. T'aint only the business side of it, either. I wondered for a long time why they ran away when they saw me, but, now I know. It was because of you. And now I know I can't have things like that; I got kids to think of. This is their home, and they'll want friends. Besides, it ain't healthy, no matter how much money you've got, to have everybody's hand against you. I can't let my kids grow up where every breath they take in their lungs is full of pizen. No, ma'am!

"I don't go around with my heart bleedin' over the trouble folks get into on account of their own damfoolishness. But when somethin' like this happens, like this here flood, it ain't nobody's fault. And everybody's got to help. It's just plain human decency.

"They got young uns in there, like mine. Young uns that ain't been eatin' regular. Aunt Betsy's over there now, takin' care of one that mightn't live until mornin'. I looked at them kids, and I thought, what if they was mine? If you'd any of that heart I thought you used to have, you'd be over there, too.

"But all these things tonight just made me realize that they wasn't nothin' in themselves. They just made me sort of realize what's wrong between you and me. What's always been wrong. I always knew you had funny ideas that wasn't connected with real livin', but I thought you sort of loved me, underneath. And so, I held on, standin' lots of things no other man'd stand from his woman.

"But now I know that things'll never be any better. You wouldn't let 'em be better. You've got somethin' in you that'd never let you be happy, and wouldn't let you let anybody else be happy. What it is I don't know. And somehow, now, I don't care. That's somethin' you got to get over yourself, or die in. It's—it's a sort of spell on you.

"I didn't think you hated me. But I saw it in your eyes

tonight. I didn't need any of your words. I saw it plainly.

"And so we can't be a man and his woman any more. T'aint my doin'; it's yours. You'll go on makin' a misery for yourself, but, by God! you ain't goin' to make a misery for me and the young uns no more! I'm agoin' to see to that, myself.

"You ain't got any kin, there ain't a soul that'll take you in. If there was, I'd say to you, 'Go away, where you won't have to see me, pore soul, and where you'd have your sickness by yourself.' But, you ain't got nobody. So, I want you to stay here; I won't ever bother you agin.

"I'm sorry for you, Maggie. Right sorry. Livin' here all these years in your misery when you might've been happy, if it wasn't for your own self. You miss a lot, Maggie. You used to like to run around, and sit on the hills; seemed like you was part of them, part of everythin' that growed, and I loved you for it. You've lost that, too.

"Seems like only God can help you. I can't. I tried. T'wasn't any use. And that's all I got to say."

He looked at her steadily. For the first time she saw compassion and real, impersonal grief in his eyes. While he had been speaking it seemed to her that the conflagration within herself had grown to terrible proportions, that she was being consumed in it. She could not endure the anguish of it. Worse, she did not understand it. She wanted to cry out to him: "John! Don't leave me! I'll die if you leave me!" But she could not. There were so many things clamoring in her to be said, but now that they had become articulate she was only terrified, dumfounded. She made herself speak, and loathed herself for the words.

"You thought I didn't know, John, but I've known for three weeks that Bill King came back, that's he's staying with his folks until they get out in the spring. And you never said anything to him—"

He looked at her for a long moment before replying. Then he smiled sadly.

"Maggie, that wasn't what you wanted to say. Perhaps, one of these days, you'll say it to me. But until you do, we won't be seein' much of each other. All I can do is wait. Good night."

He picked up his blankets and went out of the room, closing the door gently behind him.

For a long time Margaret stood where he had left her, in the center of the room. She stared at the closed door. It was as if a part of her had run out after John, screaming wordlessly.

Finally she flung herself across the bed, limp, and deadened. When dawn came into the cold room, she was still lying there, fully clothed, in a deep sleep of exhaustion, her hair strewn about her.

Chapter Nineteen

WHEN MARGARET CAME DOWNSTAIRS in the late morning the house was quiet. John was gone. The children were in the kitchen with the girls, coaxing cookies. A fire was crackling in the dining room and she sat beside it, feeling utterly drained. Mary brought her some coffee and biscuits. The girl looked tired and cross, and she thumped the dishes on the table. She put a letter down beside them.

"Coffee ain't so good," she mumbled, without looking at Margaret. "But you didn't come down right away." She went out of the room.

Margaret picked up the letter. It was from her Aunt Susan. Listlessly, she tore it open. Another envelope fell out. She stared at it blankly. There was a note in Susan Blodgett's scrawl.

"Ralph is here visiting me, and he wants me to send you this letter. I ain't got nothing else to say."

It seemed to Margaret, as she ripped open the other envelope, that she could never tear through the stubborn paper, that eternities swung dreamily about her until she had spread open the paper. Even then, the letters blurred before her eyes for moments.

"Dear Margaret: I received your letter. I knew it would come some day and so I have waited. You took longer than I thought you would. I have come down to see my mother and will be here for two days. Won't you come to me at once? For obvious reasons, I cannot come to you. R.B."

Margaret read the letter over and over before she understood it. Then she thrust it quickly between the coals in the fireplace. She was breathing hard as she ran to the window; she was vaguely surprised to feel herself trembling. There was no sign of rain though the sky was low. She caught up a shawl and ran out to the barn. The ground was brown and slimy under her feet and she slipped once of twice.

Several men, refugees, were in the barn too, waiting with small pails for milk for their children. They were talking to John, chewing the tobacco he had given them, and spitting. They were all gaunt and dirty. They stared at Margaret as she came in, then looked aside. She ran up to John, breathing hard.

"John! I just got a letter from Aunt Susie! She's—she's sick, and she wants me to come down at once. I'd like to have the trap in about an hour, and I'll drive it down there myself!"

He waited a full minute before he replied, and then he said slowly, "It's twenty miles, Mag. And the road's bad, even if the flood ain't been goin' down that way. Wait till evenin', and I'll drive you down, myself."

"No. No! I've got to go, now. Twenty miles isn't bad."

He looked at her steadily. Haggard though she was, life glittered on her face, and her lips usually so dry and pale, were moist and glowing.

Funny, he thought, saw Si Rowe yesterday and he didn't say nothin' about old Susie bein' sick. But—but, and it seemed to him that a jagged flash of lightning struck him apart, he did say somethin' about Ralph Blod gett bein' down to see his ma for a couple days. Ralph Blodgett. So that's it! I been a fool for years!

Nothing of what he thought showed in his stolid expression. But he felt physically sick. He wet his lips.

"It's a long way, Mag. And bad goin'. It'll take you most all day. I don't like you goin' alone, but seems like you're set on it. Are you takin' both the young uns with you?"

"No," said Margaret. She did not look at him directly. "I don't want to take either of them. It's—it's bad going, as you say. I'll leave them here, and I'll be back tomorrow."

"That's good," commented John with apparent easiness. He felt moisture pricking his scalp. "I been thinkin'

of runnin' in to Whitmore today or tomorrow mornin'. I
need some things. Got to see what they think up there
'bout me runnin' for mayor next year, too. I'll take both
the young uns."

Margaret, who had already started for the door, halted.
"But the river's up, John."

"The bridge at Big Bend's all right. It'll hold. And the
river's been goin' down for three days. It'll be good for the
kids to take a ride with their dad, and the wimin folk
bein' so busy and all, I don't like to leave 'em here in the
way." Margaret was already outside now, so he called,
"If Ole Susie needs anythin', let me know."

Margaret did not answer; in fact, she had not heard.
She ran back to the house. She was startled and annoyed
to see Miss Betsy in the dining room, rubbing her dry
hands before the blaze.

She turned as Margaret entered. She had been about
to speak, but at the sight of Margaret's thin face, vivid as
it had not been for years, she stopped.

"Aunt Betsy," said Margaret, "I've got to go away, until tomorrow night. To my aunt's. She's sick. I can't take
the children, and I wonder if you'd sort of keep an eye
on them—"

"Going away? And we're short-handed, with all those
folks in the old house. I came over to ask you to help.
Two of the children are very sick over there, and I
thought you'd have the Christian decency to help us. I
haven't been to bed yet, and the hired girls are all played
out. They're not mules."

Margaret removed her shawl, clutched it tightly in her
hands. Now that the glow was fading, she looked ill. But
resolute, terribly resolute, as though she had at last got a
hold upon life and would not let go. Something frantic
sprang into her eyes.

"I'm sorry. I've got to go to my aunt. I'll be back tomorrow and help."

She left the room; her hurried feet stumbled on the
stairs. She was throwing articles into a small carpetbag.
The children came into her room, and her voice, as
she told them to leave, had something wild in it.

When Margaret came downstairs in her short brown jacket and thick brown skirts, her bonnet tied neatly under her chin, and carrying her bag, John was already standing at the side door beside the horse and trap. With burning impatience she allowed him to tuck the rug about her knees and listened fumingly to his advice. She did not notice how unusually quiet his voice was. She did not know that he stared after her for a long time, as she drove away over the muddy road.

Margaret drove swiftly, almost recklessly, now that she was on the highway. The air was chilly and dark, and there was no sound but that of the horse and the straining wheels. Even the houses they passed were huddled and gray, half-drowned, though this section had been spared the worst of the flood. Smoke hung over desolate eaves. It might have been late twilight instead of midday. For miles Margaret met no one, saw no one. All she heard was the riotous beating of her heart, the humming of her thoughts.

She was going to see Ralph.

She felt delirious, unreal. Her hands, in their thick gloves, were hot with nervousness. She slapped the reins on the horse's back; she soared out of the trap, out of her body, flew to the farmhouse eight miles away.

She had forgotten to bring any food, and two hours later she was surprised at the pangs of hunger she felt. The horse was becoming exhausted; the skies were darkening rapidly. Then slow drops thrummed on the roof of the trap.

The horse began to limp, and she still had nearly two miles to go. It was already twilight, a twilight of inundated and silent horrors. She was shivering with cold and nervousness. She passed a cabin, standing alone in a shallow lake of mud and water. She stopped the horse and shouted. After an interminable time, filled with the sound of the relentless rain and wind, a door opened and a young boy came out onto the stoop.

"Hey, you!" shouted Margaret, her voice thick in the wet air. "My horse's got a stone. Help me, will you?"

The boy went back into the house. He was gone a long

time. Then he came out again in hip boots. Margaret watched his slow approach apprehensively. She had not realized the waters were so high. He came abreast of the trap; he was pitifully thin. He lifted the horse's foot, removed the stone, all without a word. Then he looked at Margaret. She fumbled in her bag, drew out a silver cartwheel, and gave it to him. He was still staring stupidly at it as she drove away.

Night had fallen before she reached her aunt's home. She was shuddering, wet through, the horse limping again, the rug half out of the trap. She was conscious of total exhaustion which even anticipation could not lighten.

The house was shut and grim, but a dim light showed in one window. It was several minutes before she had strength to shout and even then her voice was weak. The door opened reluctantly, and two men came out. They were just indistinct figures against the lamplight behind them, but Margaret knew that one of them was Ralph. She began to tremble again, and tears fell over her face.

One of the figures began to run towards her. It was Silas Rowe. He stared up at her in the darkness.

"Well, I swan!" he muttered. "Ralph, it's Maggie Hamilton," he called over his shoulder. The other figure came to the extreme edge of the stoop, hesitated, then stopped. But his voice, light and eager, floated out over the ground.

"Margaret!"

Silas lifted Margaret out of the trap. She was numb, and cried out as the thick water oozed up about her ankles and her cramped limbs straightened themselves. "Of all the damn foolishness!" growled Silas. He jerked his thumb toward the house. "Go on in. I'll tend to this pore beast." Margaret began to walk, weak and half fainting. Ralph stood on the stoop, hands outstretched to her impatiently.

"Hurry, Margaret, hurry! Why are you walking so slowly?"

She walked slowly, indeed, suffering. Mrs. Blodgett had joined her son, wrapped in her shawl. She shrilled:

"Whatever! You comin' out this way after the flood and all, Maggie Hamilton! You ain't got no sense! And alone! You're a fool, Maggie Hamilton!"

In a nightmare, Margaret heard herself gasping. She thought that she would never reach the stoop. Even when she did, and Ralph grasped her hand and pulled her up, it seemed to her that she was still walking in the darkness, with the cold waters about her ankles.

He put his arm around her and led her into the house, Susan Blodgett pounding ridicule in the rear. It was blessedly warm in the crowded farmhouse; a fire leapt and danced redly. Margaret fell into a chair, she felt Ralph pulling off her wet boots, felt Susan tugging roughly at her jacket and bonnet. She began to cry. Through the shimmering of her tears she looked down at Ralph, at her feet. He did not seem familiar to her. She was conscious only of a great tiredness, of a desire for the power of a strong arm, for a voice that would comfort her. She cried harder.

Susan pushed something into her hands, still scolding. It was a cup of hot coffee. Margaret drank gulpingly.

"You look a sight!" said Susan. "Like a drowned pup. Served you right if you'd have got stuck somewhere in the mud. Of all things! Here, now, rest a while, and I'll go out in the kitchen and see if I can get you some vittles."

She went out, grumbling, Margaret looked at Ralph. He smiled. He was standing beside her. For the first time she noticed that he was holding her hand. His hand was soft and fine, unfamiliar after years of John's calloused grip. She felt the pressure of a ring on his finger. She stared at him blankly.

She hardly recognized him. Though he was still in his middle twenties, he had put on weight and through the fine broadcloth of his clothing he bulked larger than Margaret remembered. There was even a fold of soft flesh over the edge of his high white collar and red silk cravat. The fine modeling of his face, too, was obscured by heaviness. For some reason she thought of the almost Grecian nose of the old Ralph. When he touched her wet eyes with his fine linen handkerchief, she caught a whiff of scent, and the musky odor caught in her throat.

He, in his turn, studied her. His first thought was: She's grown older, yes. We both have, but the years have been kind to Margaret. She's still beautiful. It's because she's suffered that there's something haunted about her. It's because she hasn't forgotten me, no more than I've forgotten her. And he sighed.

"Margaret," he said softly, "I've so much I want to say to you." But she only stared at the fire, her hands wrung hard together in her lap. Yes, she thought, it was almost the same voice, the voice that had been filled with troubled glory. But now it was serene, satisfied. She looked at him wearily, tried to smile.

"I had a lot to say, too," she said faintly. He smiled, then bent and kissed her cheek. It was very cold. He felt cheated; all these years she had been a vital and glowing memory to him, a heightened creature of splendor. This tired, white-faced woman with drawn lips had come to him instead. A faint anger began to stir in him, a sort of indignation that she had cheated him.

Susan came in with a plate of cold potatoes, fried pork and beans, and a smaller plate with a flabby piece of pie upon it. Margaret looked at these offerings, and then at Ralph, so grotesquely out of place in that plain and ugly farmhouse "settin' room" that she wanted to laugh madly. Ralph had left her on that hilltop so many years ago, and he would never return. Her disappointment was like acrid poison in her mouth. Mingled with it was an enormous self-contempt, enormous laughter turned against herself. She had been dreaming of a dead man.

Susan stood fussily near Margaret until the latter pretended to eat. Margaret's hand shook with complete exhaustion; the food nauseated her.

"I must say, Maggie," said Susan fretfully, "that I don't see how you got over here. In all that mud. And the bridges down, and the flood over everythin'. Land, you must have wanted to come a heap to half drowned yourself."

"I did want to come," said Margaret in her tired voice.

Ralph smiled at her significantly. She tried to smile in return; she felt only ludicrous. So she asked Ralph about Lydia and the little girl. Ralph sighed gently before answering; he looked at Margaret meaningly when he spoke of his wife. He implied to Margaret that Lydia had never, could never, take her place. Only Margaret counted, the girl who had walked hand in hand with him through this valley. However, beneath his words, she saw that he was not at all discontent. "It's only a pose," she thought with bitter amusement.

It occurred to her, sharply, that he had not asked about her at all, that he had never mentioned John or the children. He was not interested. She remembered, now, that he had never been interested in what had concerned her. How had she forgotten that?

Suddenly it seemed to her that this man was a caricature; that he was something to weep over. This was not Ralph; Ralph had gone away and never come back. This was not even a man, only a stranger blurred in the image of Ralph, a stranger without a heart and only a second-rate mind.

She looked at him. "Have you seen anything of the flood country?"

He was puzzled and slightly offended. "What? Flood country? No, I haven't seen the flood country. It's bad enough out here. But I was worried about mother in this dreadful region, so I came." Susan beamed on him fondly, clicked her needles. But into the dark scarred places of Margaret the painful new blood was rushing, healing but agonizing.

She said, "You know, of course, that Pa was killed by a horse. Mashed. You would hardly have recognized his face." She watched him closely as she spoke. Ralph's brows wrinkled.

"Yes. I was sorry to hear about Uncle Peter. But, Margaret, need you describe it so realistically?"

"Death is realistic, Ralph," she heard herself saying. "Just as realistic as life. Perhaps more."

He stared at her. Her face had become flushed, her eyes were sparkling. Here was the old Margaret, strong with vitality and anger. He could not be angry with her. He, too, had an enchantment he wished to keep.

"I ain't asked you yet, Maggie," said Susan tightly, "but how's John? Much damage done to his land down there?"

Margaret turned her eyes upon her. "John," she said slowly. "John is well. No, the farm isn't hurt much." She continued to look at her aunt, but into her eyes leaped a fire. John! Why, John was her husband, steady, inarticulate, forever there! She loved him. She had always loved him! How had she forgotten that? Suddenly, desperately, she wanted him. She half rose, then fell back, shaking. But she was filled with joy and incredible satisfaction. What a fool she had been!

She thought of the wasted years, the silly years, when she might have been happy with her husband and her children! Miss Betsy had known what was in her mind; no wonder she had despised her. But, no more than she despised herself.

Thank God, it's not too late! she thought humbly.

She marveled at her monumental blindness. She was seized with a passion of longing to see John, to hear his voice, to feel the touch of his hand. How miserable she had made him! She had robbed herself of life, of joy, of the beauty of reality. But, it was not too late. Thank God, it was not too late!

Susan, yawning, stood up. "Well, seems like it's time to go to bed. You better go, too, Maggie. I'll fix up a room for you. The one at the head of the stairs, cross from mine and Si's."

Margaret and Ralph, left alone, looked at each other. He reached over, and took her hand. "Margaret," he said softly. She merely smiled. But she was compassionate; she must rid him of his enchantment, too.

They heard Susan scolding as she went upstairs, followed by the growling Si. A deep silence fell upon the house. Ralph drew his chair closer to Margaret.

"Margaret. Maggie, dear. You asked me to come," he whispered.

"Yes," she said clearly. "I asked you to come. I didn't know, then, how glad I would be to see you again."

He misunderstood, of course. He kissed the palm of her hand, then he looked up at her.

"Margaret, why did you do it to me? Why did you send me away, and then turn around and marry that— that country laborer, that melodramatic village squire? What had I done, Margaret?"

Why, she thought, you wouldn't have things different if you could! You wouldn't change your devoted Lydia for me, not for twice as much money! You wouldn't give up your position, your comfort, your fine gold chain and your private carriage, your publishing business, your satisfaction and security, for a dozen like me! You're acting a part.

Then, all at once, she knew that he believed himself sincere, that to show him his real insincerity would be to deal him a cruel blow. She had really hurt him once; she could not do it again. She said gently:

"I knew I could never make you happy, Ralph. I knew what I was, inside. So I married John to save you— I thought I was doing the best thing. I wanted to have you forgive me."

Suddenly he knelt before her, took her hands and held them to the smoothness of his cheeks. She had to check an instinctive recoil.

"Margaret," he said in a choked voice, "I want you to know this. I forgive you. I forgave you long ago. I knew that in some way you were being wise and kind. You were always that.

"Margaret, through all these years, you have been more to me than anyone else. I love Lydia, yes, but not the way I have always loved you, and still love you. When I write my poems, I write them for you. You give my life substance and beauty. I'll go away, and I'll never see you. I know that. But you will continue to give me substance and beauty. You will make the world lovely for me, as you have always done. You will give me your strength, as you did before. Without remembering you, without loving you, there would be nothing."

She looked blindly into the distance. She knew he spoke the truth. Yes, for the first time, he had spoken from his own depths. She knew that she could never take this illusion from him. His enchantment had been to him a refuge of lush, tree-hidden lands. It had taken the place of courage in him. It had rescued him from fear. His life and happiness depended on a lie.

She moved her hands over his face, smoothed his hair. "You have been all that to me, too, Ralph dear," she whispered. "You'll always be that to me. Perhaps you're right and we won't ever see each other again. But we'll always remember how we love each other, and it will give us courage, won't it? We'll always have that. We'll always love each other."

He held her tightly. The clock ticked; the coals fell into dimness. Ralph was silent in his happiness. But Margaret was conscious of a growing weariness. Even as he held her, she was making plans to slip away in the morning. She wanted to rest, so that she could drive relentlessly. She wanted to go back to John, to see him, to hear him. Even as she murmured to Ralph, her eyes were bright with the thought of her husband.

Finally he released her. He was very pale. He kissed her hands slowly and tenderly, while she smiled down at him. She let him kiss her lips, and she thought, Did we really lie together that night on the hill? She felt shame and disgust, and so kissed him lightly.

Chapter Twenty

SILAS ROWE HAD JUST SET his lantern down in the acridly pungent barn when he heard a step behind him. It was barely half-past five of a raw gray morning, drifting with vapors. He was amazed to see Margaret Hobart, fully dressed and bonnetted behind him. She smiled at him in the yellowish lantern light.

"Si, will you harness my horse for me? I'm leaving right away."

"Eh?" he grunted. He put a thick hand to his ear and scratched it.

"Please hurry, Si. I've got to go home. I can't wait another minute."

Silas glanced involuntarily at the house. There was not a glimmer of light showing in its slumbering huddle.

"Ain't you stayin' for breakfast?" he asked.

"I've been in the kitchen and I drank well onto a quart of milk, ate five cold biscuits and butter, and a piece of pie. Isn't that enough?"

"Susie know you're agoin'?" he persisted.

"Oh—what does it matter?" she demanded impatiently. "No, she doesn't know I'm going! You tell her I had to go. Tell that to Ralph, too. He'll understand."

"Bet Susie won't," muttered Silas, with a half leer at Margaret.

He hitched the horse for her. She swung into the trap lightly and caught up the reins. Silas lifted the lantern; she looked like a young girl, he thought, all asparkle and aquiver, instead of a woman going out before dawn into a desolate and dangerous country.

"Been rainin' a lot last night," he said warningly. "Mebbe the cricks are up agin and the bridges down. Then what'll you do?"

"Swim!" she laughed. She cracked the whip and the horse, his breath rising in clouds, felt his way carefully in the half darkness. The trap crept out toward the public road. Moisture drummed ceaselessly on the roof; Margaret could hear the sucking of the mud around the horse's hoofs. Beyond these sounds, and the sound of the horse and the creaking wheels, there was nothing. It gave Margaret a sense of unreality, as though she alone were alive in a dead world. She passed the dark angular shapes of farmhouses; no lights showed in them, though in the east the muddy skies were turning a faint yellow.

A fever was burning in Margaret, running along her flesh. Her body felt rigid and too intensely alive. She lost a sense of her surroundings, thought only of her return. She would go to John and look at him simply and put her hand in his, saying "Forgive me, John. I've been a fool." And he would look at her in his steady way, and then he would take her in his arms. He would ask nothing, say nothing, but she would lay her head on his strong shoulder, close her eyes, and be at peace. All at once she began to sing wordlessly, in a wild, improvised tune, her voice muffled in the fog. She laughed aloud, whistled as she had not done since her marriage, laughed again when rain dashed into her face.

It can't be more than seven, she thought at last. If I keep on this way without any accidents I'll be home before three o'clock. She passed over a small wooden bridge. The horse was obviously frightened, and had to be whipped to go over it. The waters washed over the rotten boards, and the bridge shook and wavered under the weight of horse and vehicle. It was full daylight now, but a dark and threatening one. She passed farmhouses where dispirited chickens huddled on stoops and even more dispirited men sloshed about in barnyards and fed dejected cattle.

Alive, now, she was full of pity and sudden heaviness of heart. The damage was too great to be alleviated much by individual effort. But she and John would do their part; whatever they had would be at the disposal of these poor wretches. She felt a surge of impersonal love and compassion. She could hardly bear the poignancy of her awakened emotions.

I might have been dead for these past years, she thought bitterly. I've let these years mean nothing to me. I've robbed myself and I've robbed John of living. I'll make it up! I'll live as I never lived before. I'll think only of making John happy, and the children.

At twelve o'clock, she reached higher land. The hills were crowding close. They were a darker brown than the muddy earth, but here and there they showed, on higher levels, the green of late grass, the thinning scarlet of small trees. And then, suddenly, the sun came out, splendid and overpowering, bursting its way through dun clouds. The hills became tawny with running light, and the earth shone and sparkled in all its small false lakes of flood water. The air became warmer, quivering with promise, and sparrows began to chirp on every tree.

After death comes life, thought Margaret, and was not ashamed to discover that she was crying. She stopped the horse and looked at the transfigured country. The standing horse dropped his head and moisture steamed from him.

The sun continued to shine, at first intermittently, and then steadily. Its joyous influence brought people out from the houses; they stared about at the ruins stupidly, then new hope showed in their quickened steps.

Margaret was coming to the higher land that marked the last miles of home. She passed whole pastures that were untouched by water, many farmhouses that were still dry and snug. The horse knew he was approaching his stable, and began to trot without the urge of the whip. The road was still terrible, full of holes and treacherous stones, but the shining countryside diverted Margaret's attention from the constant swaying and grinding of the trap. She noticed a new sweetness in the air.

She was less than a mile from home, and recognized familiar landmarks. Three men were standing talking excitedly at a gate, with agitated gestures that were alien to a reserved people. They heard Margaret approaching, and stared at her. Then they glanced at each other, and stared again.

She waved her whip at them gaily, and called, "Hi, Elmer. Hi, Tom, and Charlie!"

"Hi, Miz Hobart," they mumbled. She beamed upon them and drove on. But something made her look back; Elmer was shaking his head vociferously. "G'wan, I won't!" she heard him say. "Time enough when she gits there."

What did he mean? She turned again and looked; they were staring after her as though fascinated. A small nagging uneasiness began to gnaw at her.

She emerged now on the broad floor of the valley. In the distance she could see the white glimmer of the house. The horse began to trot again. She was passing over her own land, her own rich acres, her own earth. The high waters had retreated completely; because they had never risen very high here. The grass was in its last greenness; even the hills were a soft green. She saw everything with new eyes. She was like someone who had been away from home for many years and was returning, noticing every detail with tenderness and affection. She felt herself at last, again, one with the earth, with all things.

Half a mile, a quarter of a mile. She saw a group of men and women standing in the road ahead. They heard the wheels of the trap and turned. Immediately they were silent, staring at her emptily. She wanted to call out to them, I've come home! See, I'm home! She waved her whip at them.

When she came abreast of them, she saw that one of the women was crying, and that she hid her face from Margaret. The other women glanced aside, wetting their lips. The men fumbled in their pockets, reddened.

Sudden fear fell upon her. "What's the matter?" she demanded, leaning out of the trap, her face going white. "Is someone hurt?"

For several long seconds there was only silence. Then one of the women came toward Margaret. Her expression was sad and fearful.

"You been away, Miz Hobart. Ain't you heard?"

"Heard what?" cried Margaret. "What's the matter?"

The woman glanced at her companions as though asking help, and then she mumbled, "Miz Hobart, I ain't likin' to tell you this, but seems like nobody else will. Johnny Hobart's been hurt—bad. You'd best go home right quick."

Margaret stared at her dumbly. "Hurt?" she whispered, swallowing hard. No, dear God, this was not true! She was coming home to him! "Hurt? Do you mean—"

"No, Miz Hobart. He ain't dead. Yet." Helplessly, she looked at the others. "But that ain't all. You'd best go home and find out, yourself."

Still gazing at the woman Margaret lifted her whip and struck the horse. The horse leapt, the trap almost turned over, then animal and vehicle ran and bumped wildly, madly, down the road. They looked after her; she was crouching, slashing at the horse; they could see the insane rise and fall of her whip, the leaping, straining back of the tired animal.

The countryside, so beaming with light only a moment ago, now became a hell-lit nightmare land to her; it seemed to her that the horse ran only in one spot. She was not conscious that she was making that raw and groaning noise she heard dimly. Her arm did not tire in its flailing.

She could see nothing but old Margot's face, and a loud cry burst from her.

"Granny, don't let anything happen to him! Hold him; don't let him go! Granny, please!"

The house was only a hundred yards away. As in a dream she saw the knots of men and women, and children. When the horse and trap roared up, they looked at Margaret somberly. Reaching the gate, she leapt down, flung aside the reins. Someone opened the gate for her; she saw only a monstrous vision of pitying faces. She ran toward the house, caught her foot on her skirts, and fell to her hands and knees. Before anyone could reach her, she was up again, not even limping, though blood smeared her palms. Her hair fell from its coils and tumbled down her back. Everyone stood aside to let this wild-faced woman pass; there was something in her expression that frightened them. She reached the door, they heard her cry out, and then she vanished.

"Looks like Maggie Hamilton's come down from her high horse this time," said the acid voice of a woman.

"Shet up!" a man cried fiercely, and there was an approving murmur.

Once in the hall, Margaret began to call in a hoarse, strained voice. "John! Mary! Mabel! Aunt Betsy!"

The dim quiet of the hall floated around her. She could hear low voices upstairs. She ran to the foot of the stairs and started to climb, her legs bending under her. But before she was halfway up, Miss Betsy appeared at the top. The old woman had thought of this moment with a certain bitter hatred, but now, looking down at Margaret, her hair about her, her face mad, blood on her hands, the hatred died away with only compassion left. She ran as lightly as a girl down the stairs and put her arm about the younger woman.

"Margaret," she said quietly, "my poor girl. No, you can't go up there yet. I want to talk to you. No, Margaret, please don't fight me. Listen to me. John is sleeping now; I've got to talk to you before you see him."

Margaret clutched her savagely, hope in her eyes. "He's not dead?" she moaned.

"No," said Miss Betsy gravely, and sighed. Her eyes filled with tears. "Not dead, Margaret. He won't die, we hope. It's his leg. Broken, and he's got a deep wound in the head, and he's badly bruised. But Dr. Brewster said he'll get well. Come with me, Margaret, into the parlor. I must talk to you."

Margaret had begun to sob; she collapsed against Miss Betsy; her eyes closed. But she could still walk; she felt herself being led away; she felt herself being put gently into a chair. Through the mists she could see the sunlight on the stiff white curtains. She cried uncontrollably. Miss Betsy stood beside her for a moment; her own face was very white. Then she pulled a chair up beside the younger woman.

"Margaret," she said quietly. "I always thought you

were brave; I knew you were brave. You aren't a fool. If you were, you wouldn't be here now. You wouldn't feel the way you do. So I can talk to you without mincing words. You've got to know. If you were a weakling I'd let you know gradually. But you're strong."

Something in her manner quieted Margaret, but only increased the dread she felt. She dropped her hands from her face, looked at Miss Betsy stonily.

"Tell me," she said hoarsely. "I don't care what happened so long as John is going to live. I can stand everything."

"Yes, I believe you can stand it. Margaret, about three hours ago John took Gregory and Dickie with him to Whitmore." She paused. For a moment she struggled for breath. "They went in the buggy. He didn't want to leave the children alone, seeing as how I was over in the old house and had my hands full with two sick babies, and the girls were tired out. So he took the children.

"No one knows yet just what happened, Margaret. But a little way behind the buggy Bill King was riding to town on his horse. Seth Holbrooks and Mrs. Holbrooks were about an eighth of a mile behind Bill. Well, John rode over the bridge at Big Bend, the only bridge that hadn't been washed out. And when he and the children were halfway over, the bridge went down.

"You know how the creek's been during the last couple of weeks. Like a torrent, full of tree trunks, rushing along like something crazy—" She stopped.

A pang of mortal agony twisted Margaret, and her hands writhed in her lap. "Go on," she whispered. Her dry lips moved.

"Well, Margaret, we don't know just what happened. But John said to me, when he could, that there was no use trying to save both children at once. He said he thought of you, even when he was fighting in that water, trying to swim against the current that he must save Dickie for you. So he caught at poor little Dickie and tried to swim with him. A tree trunk came along, dashing and swirling, and he got between it and the boy. That's when his leg was broken. But somehow, thanks to God, he caught hold of the roots of a tree, and held himself and Dickie above water until Seth Holbrooks had come up, and could drag them out.

"And now, Margaret, only a little more, God help you. Bill King had come up, almost on John's heels. He saw what was happening; he saw poor little Gregory's head, and he dived in, boots and coat and all, to save him. Seth Holbrooks said that he saw him take hold of the baby, who was screaming for John, and that he thought everything would be all right. But another trunk came along, and hit Bill. He struggled against it, kept on swimming though he was covered with blood, still holding on to Gregory. And then," she said softly, turning aside for a moment, "they both went down. They were out in the middle of the water, and nothing could be done. They didn't come up again."

She turned to Margaret again, weeping. But Margaret was staring into space. Her hands were still in her lap. There was no moisture in her eyes.

"Don't look like that, Maggie," whispered Miss Betsy, putting her arms about her. "God was good. Dickie is all right, though a little bruised. He's in bed. John will get well, we hope. And we must remember that Bill King gave his life to try to save poor little Gregory. We must remember that."

Margaret turned her blind eyes to her. "Nothing matters," she said clearly. "Nothing matters. Just so long as I still have John."

And then she stood up. "I killed Gregory, Aunt Betsy. If I had not gone away, the children would have stayed with me. Gregory would be here, shouting in this room. I killed him. Don't you see that?"

Miss Betsy stood up, too. "But, Margaret," she said, "If you had not gone, you wouldn't have come back, really come back, to John. You see, we knew why you had gone. And when you came back, I knew you had come back to your husband. I knew you had come back when I saw your face, come back in your mind and in your heart."

Chapter Twenty-one

IT WAS NIGHT before they let her see John. They were all amazed at her quietness. She had just waited until she could see John, rocking by the fire with little Dickie, whom they had brought downstairs to her, had put in her lap. She seemed to derive comfort from him. Sometimes she seemed to listen; they knew she was listening for Gregory.

Then they let her go up to John who had awakened. She went with slow and steady steps into his room, their room. The firelight glowed on the hearth and a dim light burned beside the bed. He lay with closed eyes, looking close to death, his big body ridged under the quilts. There was a bloodstained bandage about his head. He did not open his eyes until Margaret stood beside him, and then for a long time he stared at her as though trying to see her through mists.

"Maggie," he whispered through bruised lips.

She knelt down beside him, laid her cheek against his shoulder. "Forgive me, John," she said. "Just forgive me."

His bruised arm moved, feebly enclosed her. His mouth touched her head. "There ain't nothin' to forgive, Maggie, seein' that you came back to me."

The others left them alone, closed the door softly behind them.

"Maggie," said John. "I've thought about lots of things, lyin' here while they thought I was asleep. And everythin' came clear to me. We both been wrong. It took this," and his features writhed for a moment, "all this, to show us. I ain't goin' to speak of the baby; I can't, just now. But, somehow, it took it all to show us. I ain't sorry. You mustn't be. We've got a long life to live yet, you and me. Together. That's all I care about, that we'll be together."

"Together, John," she answered. "Always together."

She knew that there were months ahead of physical and mental agony, of remembering Gregory, of listening for him. Of a thousand things they would never be able to speak about. But even then, knowing this, she could put her mouth on John's sweetly, and feel peace.

THE END
of a novel by
Taylor Caldwell

The Gold Medal seal on this book means it has never been published as a book before. To select an original book that you have not read before, look for the Gold Medal seal.

25c — EXCITING ORIGINAL NOVELS — 25c

We'll be glad to send any of these never-before-published Gold Medal novels to you direct by mail.

Simply follow the directions at the end of this list.

226. **OF TENDER SIN** *David Goodis*
A boy's love for his sister torments his adult life, causing him to seek in strange places childhood's haunting love.

228. **APPOINTMENT IN PARIS** *Fay Adams*
She was very young, very American, very innocent. Paris, city of light—and shadow—took her by the hand for the dangerous journey into love.

232. **WOMAN SOLDIER** *Arnold Rodin*
Fierce, passionate Darya—by day the avenging angel of her mountain home, by night half-devil, half-woman of the earth.

234. **THE SHARP EDGE** *Richard Himmel*
From the bright lights of fame, they fled into the dangerous bypaths of love, and found they could run from everything except themselves.

238. **UNCLE GOOD'S GIRLS** *John Faulkner*
Join Uncle Good and his girls on a hell-raising election day in the *Cabin Road* country.

240. **THE DAMNED** *John D. MacDonald*
"I wish I had written this book," says Mickey Spillane. Read it and you'll see why.

241. **SAVAGE INTERLUDE** *Dan Cushman*
Greed for gold and a golden girl lured Crawford through the steaming jungle, but always blocking his path was the deadly Hammer.

246. **THE SCARLET VENUS** *Chalmers Green*
Tennessee was her name. To love her was to hate her and to hate her was to die.

250. **DARK INTRUDER** *Vin Packer*
Father and daughter rode roughshod, thinking alike, talking alike, feeling alike; too arrogant to hear the whispers. By the author of *Spring Fire*.

252. **SATAN TAKES THE HELM** *Calvin Clements*
The young captain wanted the ship. The aged owner's beautiful wife wanted the captain. They loved and schemed and hated. A great sea story of today.

254. **ABOUT DOCTOR FERREL** *Day Keene*
He was a successful doctor, but for a greedy little waif he broke his doctor's oath. By the author of *Home Is the Sailor.*

256. **STREET OF THE LOST** *David Goodis*
Here is the story of Ruxton Street, in the city's lowest slums. A street of prostitutes, workers, and dope pushers. But a street where people live and love as they do on any back street in your own home town.

258. **ESCAPE TO LOVE** *Edward S. Aarons*
They were alone on the warm, shining beach—the beautiful young girl and the man who loved her. Then came the gunshot that plunged them into terror. So much to live, so little time.

262. **WHO EVIL THINKS** *Richard Glendinning*
Dan's world was his beautiful young wife. Then fabulous Tony Maile came along. His millions could buy anything—even Dan's wife. With his world crashing, Dan fought for life and sanity—and for love.

264. **BRENDA** *Lehi Zane*
There was the simple, pious valley town. And there was luscious, lustful Brenda. Tragedy rode on the wings of passion when good and evil clashed.

266. **PLUNDER** *Benjamin Appel*
Joe and Blackie, two tough GI's just out of the stockade, hit war-ravaged Manila like a typhoon. Black markets. Women for the homesick Yanks. A sweet-money town for Joe and Blackie. A bitter, savage novel of our time by one of our time's great authors.

269. **THE DEVIL DRIVES** *Robert Ames*
This is the story of Kim, who thirsted after gold and despised the weak husband who could not give it to her. And of four killers who had figured all the angles—all except Kim.

273. **UNHOLY FLAME** *Olga Rosmanith*
Beautiful Lissa sought to find peace in the strange, macabre cult of Suliman. But was he saint or devil? An adventure into the forbidden—as fantastic as it is terrifying.

274. **BEYOND DESIRE** *Richard Himmel*
Here is the novel of a passionate quest for a lost manhood—as it could be written only by Richard Himmel, brilliant author of *The Sharp Edge.*

276. **MOUNTAIN GIRL** *Cord Wainer*
She ruled the mountain town through her strange fascination for men. Only tough, handsome Ricky threatened her power, and she swore she would conquer him—or kill him.

278. **THAT FRENCH GIRL** *Joseph Hilton*
The amazing story of a French *fille de joie*, who married a millionaire and taught an American community morals and manners.

279. **THE BIG GUY** *Wade Miller*
The story of dynamic, brutal Joe Drum, who beat his way to the top of gangdom and ruled supreme—until a woman found his fatal weakness.

281. **SWAMP BRAT** *Allen O'Quinn*
They fought for a man's love—the lady and the girl of the swamp. An exciting novel of the country Faulkner made famous.

283. **THE FIRE GODDESS** *Sax Rohmer*
Sumuru, witch of the world, in her forbidden fortress on a voodoo-ridden West Indian isle plots world domination. The old master at his best.

285. **TOO RICH TO DIE** *H. Vernor Dixon*
The story of a man with too much money and too much fame who faced humiliation and death for the woman he loved.

286. **HELL HATH NO FURY** *Charles Williams*
In the sleepy southern town, a woman's hatred spun a web of evil. The new novel by the author of HILL GIRL and BIG CITY GIRL.

288. **MAGGIE—HER MARRIAGE** *Taylor Caldwell*
She was made of earth and air and she turned her marriage into a fiery hell. By the world-famous author of THIS SIDE OF INNOCENCE.

In case your local dealer cannot supply you, send 25 cents for each copy desired, plus 5 cents per book for handling and mailing, to

GOLD MEDAL BOOKS

Fawcett Place,   Greenwich, Conn.

PLEASE NOTE: Canadian orders not accepted.